HARVEY DUCKMAN PRESENTS...

VOL. 1

A collection of sci-fi, fantasy, steampunk and horror short stories

6e

Published in paperback in 2019 by Sixth Element Publishing

Sixth Element Publishing
Arthur Robinson House
13-14 The Green
Billingham TS23 1EU
Tel: 01642 360253
www.6epublishing.net

ISBN 978-1-912218-54-7

British Library Cataloguing in Publication Data. A catalogue record for this book is available from the British Library.

Printed in Great Britain.

CONTENTS

FOREWORD

Welcome. I am Harvey Duckman.

In this assemblage, I am presenting the first in a series of collected works of suspense and mystery in the genres of science fiction, fantasy, horror and steampunkery, called, oddly enough, Harvey Duckman Presents…

I neither write nor tell these stories but present them for your own delectation, something in the nature of an accomplice to a crime not yet committed.

You may be asking yourself "Who is Harvey Duckman?" but perhaps a more pertinent question to ask is "What is Harvey Duckman?"

Think of me as your ringmaster in this Circus of the Fantastic and the stories in which you are about to indulge are the fabulous acts, gathered in one place, from all corners of the imagination.

In our circus however there is no performance schedule. No rigid playbill. You, dearest member of the audience, may enjoy our tales in whichever order pleases you the most, or indeed the least, if your preference is such, and come and go as you wish.

But for now, dear reader, take your seat and make yourself comfortable as the curtain rises for the first installment of Harvey Duckman Presents…

GRIDLOCK
A SIMCAVALIER STORY

KATE BAUCHEREL

Cameron cursed as the alert pinged on her screen. Another traffic jam at the height of rush hour. The early Monday morning shift was hard enough to handle without a genuine emergency to deal with, and after a good weekend partying with friends she would rather be working from her cramped studio apartment. No such luck: the boss insisted that junior staff members work from the agency's headquarters. They had to earn his trust, he said. Cameron glanced around the virtually empty room, her head aching from a lack of sleep and the persistent alarms. She sighed and turned her attention to the screen, tapping expertly at a series of options as she dug deeper into the problem. Simple enough: a communication failure at a set of city centre traffic signals. The navigation systems in a hundred autocars were waiting for instructions to cross the busy intersection as angry commuters sat and seethed, recalling a golden age of self-determined driving. They wouldn't remember the pollution, the queues and delays, the accidents, or the unnecessary deaths, reflected Cameron as she rebooted the system. They only remembered their independence.

The alarms faded, and the system state indicators glowed a universal, reassuring green. Cameron leaned back in her chair and gazed at the ceiling. Time for a coffee to try and clear her head. She slouched her way over to the machine and pressed the Cappuccino button on the battered display. The machine sputtered and a jet of thick black liquid shot out at an angle, spattering Cameron's white shirt as she jumped back. Throwing her head back, she swore at the top of her voice, then marched to the nearby sink to rinse the stain away.

"Young lady, that was uncalled-for." The voice behind her made Cameron groan inwardly. The office manager, always listening and easily offended. "I will be speaking to Mr Thorp."

"Fine, Savannah," replied Cameron through gritted teeth. "Go ahead." She turned back to her task, dabbing ineffectively at the dark splashes which stained her clothes. "Tell him to replace this sodding machine while you're at it. This is the 2030s, not the bloody twentieth century." She gave up, threw the cloth into the sink, and stalked past the woman and back to her place.

The neighbouring desk was now occupied. "Playing with fire there, Cameron," said the newcomer.

"You think I care?" replied Cameron heavily. "Good weekend, Max?"

"Not bad, thanks. How has the morning been so far?"

"Comms failure at Shepherd's Bush," said Cameron.

"Another one?" Max frowned. "That's four on the bounce. Looks like you fixed it okay."

"I switched it off and on again," said Cameron with a shrug. "It's hardly rocket science. I can't find anything wrong with the system."

"You've run all the standard diagnostics?" asked Max.

"Not yet. I'll get onto it now." Cameron sat down and buried herself in her work, running through dull routines to check the integrity of the underlying code, and analysing signals from the hardware at the offending junction. Nothing unusual was flagging up. There was no sign of any fault. In theory, the systems were working perfectly. Tell that to the disgruntled commuters whose public posts and comments were lighting up the feedback board at the end of the office. The sentiment tracker was glowing a bright, angry red. The management would not be happy.

Gathering her thoughts, Cameron decided to look at the problem a whole new way. She pulled up a web connection and linked to a third-party system, glancing around to see that both Savannah and Max were pre-occupied. She was breaking every rule the company had, but it would save her hours of manual checking and pay off handsomely if her hunch was correct. She passed through the site's security protocols with ease: this was her own private domain. Sifting through the files in her library, she selected the snippet of code she was looking for, a benign worm which would run deep diagnostic tests her employers had never considered. She pulled the file through to the local servers and cut off her link to the outside world. Opening the file, she edited a few parameters, double checked the code, and closed it with a satisfied nod. With a tap on the keyboard she deployed her worm. It would burrow deep into the servers without damaging any other software, and the results would be back within the hour.

It was time to get a real coffee, Cameron decided. The office was gradually filling with staff and she wouldn't be missed.

"I'm going out for five minutes," she called to Max.

Sitting on a high stool at the window of the café, Cameron sipped contentedly at her hot foamy drink and gazed into space. Autocars and buses swept silently past, the Monday morning rush starting to ease. A few large hybrid delivery trucks trundled along the road, their engines startlingly loud. In a few years, reflected Cameron, they would all be obsolete, but for now the navigation signals relied upon by autocars in the cities were not reliable across the whole road network. It would only be a matter of time, though. She wondered how her redoubtable Aunt Vicky would handle the loss of her zippy sports car, which was barely legal even now in the rural commuter belt. She smiled faintly at the thought of her aunt whizzing around the country lanes in the low soft-top. Cameron loved her aunt, who had brought her up since she was twelve years old, and she loved the car, but she had never learned to drive it. She didn't need to. Those days had passed.

As she watched the traffic, Cameron noticed a subtle shift in the rhythm. She felt a cold shiver down her spine. The traffic flow was slowing. The truck drivers were sounding their horns. Suddenly, horrified, she heard a screech of brakes and the sound of crumpling metal. The autocars had stopped, but the truck drivers had not reacted quickly enough. Cameron drained her coffee and rushed out of the door and across the road. She ducked as a first responder drone whined overhead, weaved through the stationary vehicles, and dashed through the main doors of the office building which opened as they sensed her approach. Ignoring the elevator, she took the stairs two at a time and arrived, panting, at her desk. The place was in uproar and the boss was waiting for her, glowering.

"Silvera, in my office, now." He stalked off without waiting for an answer.

Cameron glanced helplessly at her screen. She needed to check the results from her worm's exploration of the servers, and more importantly she had to clean the code out in case it was found. It would have to wait. She tried to catch her colleague's eye, but Max was ignoring her, busy bringing the latest outage back on line. This felt bad. She sloped towards the boss's office, her heart in her mouth.

"I've had yet another complaint from Savannah about your attitude and your language, and you did not have permission to leave the building just now. You are already on a final warning. What were you thinking?"

Cameron kept her cool and stared just past the man's ear to the bright, angular abstract painting on the wall behind.

"It won't happen again, Mr Thorp."

"You're right, Cameron, it won't." He sighed. "You are extremely talented, but you don't have a future with this company. You can collect your belongings and you'll be paid for your notice period. Your system and entry access codes are being suspended now."

Cameron took a deep breath, nodded, and turned on her heel. She marched out to her desk and tapped experimentally at the screen. 'Access denied.' She picked up her bag and jacket and nodded to her neighbour.

"Bye, Max," she said wryly.

"Bye, Cam," he replied. "Sorry to see you go. Stay in touch." He turned back to his work.

Out on the street there were sirens sounding and blue lights flashing as emergency vehicles dealt with the accident. Traffic had started moving slowly again past the scene. Cameron pulled up her collar and headed in the opposite direction, towards the station.

The front door opened as Cameron reached the end of the path. A sleek black cat with grey in his muzzle strolled stiffly out and sniffed the air. Cameron bent to stroke him. "Hello Bob, you gorgeous old boy."

"Cameron, darling," exclaimed Aunt Vicky. "I thought you would be working."

Cameron straightened up and gave her aunt a

crooked smile. "Ah, well, there's been a bit of a hiccup there."

"Oh dear, Cameron. Shall I put the kettle on?"

Cameron nodded. "Thank you. There are some things I need to work out." She stepped into the house and dropped her things on a chair.

Aunt Vicky bustled into the kitchen and began to unearth mugs, milk and biscuits. "Tell me all about it, darling."

Cameron took a deep breath. "I was so bored at that place. I'm actually glad they asked me to leave, but I don't know what to do."

"I've always said you would find it hard to work for someone else, Cameron. You've had a few years' experience now. Why don't you set up on your own?"

"That's not what I mean, but it's a really good idea. I've thought about it before." Cameron picked her favourite biscuit from the box and took a bite. "I could work from home for a while. Everything I need is here."

"It would be lovely if you came back to live in the village," said Aunt Vicky warmly, "and Charlie and Sameena would probably appreciate the help, what with little Nina and the baby on the way."

"If my big brother thinks I'm going to be the live-in nanny, he has another think coming," said Cameron firmly. She shook her head and laughed, lightening the mood. "Okay, I may babysit occasionally."

"What's really worrying you, dear?"

"Well, I left my employment quite abruptly," said

Cameron, embarrassed. "I had a hunch that the system failures we were dealing with could be a clever bit of hacking that the standard diagnostics would miss. I set a routine off to dig down in to the systems, and I didn't have a chance to remove it. I could be in a lot of trouble if it's found. I was only trying to solve the problem."

Aunt Vicky pursed her lips. "That was silly, Cameron. I don't pretend to understand everything you do, but it sounds as if you did the wrong thing for the right reasons. What would have been the right thing to do?"

"I guess… report what I suspected to the boss and the national cybercrime unit and let them handle it." Cameron sighed. "I want to dig into it myself, though. If this is a hack, it's fiendishly clever."

"It's up to you, dear. I can't tell you what to do. But deal with honour, Cameron. Always take the high road." Aunt Vicky busied herself with the kettle. "Here, drink your tea."

Cameron settled at her old familiar desk in the farmhouse attic. The afternoon sun streamed through the south-facing dormer windows, dust motes dancing. The house was silent. She was alone. Charlie and Sameena didn't even know she had come home; it would be a nice surprise when they arrived back from work.

Silence was good. She needed to concentrate.

Her first task was to remove the code she had inserted into her erstwhile employer's servers. She glanced at the clock. Max would be finishing his shift about now. She crossed her fingers, opened an anonymous connection using a favourite VPN, and navigated to the company's host. She knew the systems well enough after her few months in the job to pick her way carefully to the less secure homeworking login page. She carefully entered Max's details, memorised after weeks of watching his careless typing, ignoring the nagging voice in her head that told her this was both unethical and illegal. When the familiar menus opened in front of her she realised she had been holding her breath, hoping that he hadn't changed his password. Breathing again, she started digging. She managed to find the full report from her worm. Glancing quickly at the findings she smiled in satisfaction. There was foreign code in a gaping hole that the standard diagnostics would never have picked up, and it looked as if the exploit was still active. Cameron copied every detail of the report and the attacker's code, then focused on deleting all trace of her worm. It seemed very simple, in the end. She logged off and closed the connection. Ten minutes had passed.

Now that she had covered her tracks it was time to do the decent thing. Cameron sent a message to Mr Thorp. She apologised for her behaviour. She didn't beg for her job back. She told him that she had a hunch about the outages and gave him enough apparently innocent observations to ensure that he could find and report the breach himself. If she was going to set up on her own, she would need potential clients and good references. Aunt Vicky was right; she couldn't afford to burn bridges.

Cameron was burning with curiosity as she unpacked the detail behind the hacker's attack. It was breathtaking in its elegance. The deeper she explored, the more impressed she was. Here was a piece of skilled work, not a script kiddie out for a bit of destructive fun. It was precisely constructed to cause the maximum disruption, and it would have been almost impossible to spot if she had not suspected it was there.

The light dulled as dusk fell and Cameron heard voices downstairs. She reluctantly tore herself away from the screen and ran down the stairs to greet her brother. Aunt Vicky had already briefed him. Cameron kissed her little niece, made herself a coffee, and disappeared back up to her lair with Charlie's blessing.

She wanted to know who was behind this attack. She cloaked her location and identity and ventured to corners of the web that she rarely visited, comparing snippets of the code she had found with routines for sale in underground marketplaces. She began to build up a profile of the writer, seeing new examples of the same cunning, effective work. She laughed when she traced the same perpetrator to an old breach in the database of a political party: that had been a big scandal, contributing to the fall of the government at the time. There was a picture building up of a group or an individual – more likely the latter – taking contracts for hire. The victims of each exploit were so different from one to the next that there was no clear pattern of motive. Money must be at the root of all the activity.

Cameron's concentration was broken by a noise in the dark. Her brother was climbing the attic stairs, fumbling for the light switch.

"Charlie! You made me jump."

"Do you know what time it is?" Charlie stifled a yawn. "I'd forgotten you were up here. We've eaten already, but there are some leftovers."

Cameron suddenly realised she was hungry. She glanced at the time on her personal screen. Charlie was right. It was very late.

"I'm sorry. I'm chasing a hacker."

"Aunt Vicky told me you were up to something. Have you caught them?"

"Not yet."

"Want to talk about work?" Charlie raised an eyebrow. He was very protective of his little sister, eight years his junior.

While he had settled down to run the family firm, she drifted from job to job and spent her spare time chasing wraiths in the underbelly of the world wide web. One day she would find her place, and then the world had better brace itself.

"I'll tell you all about it over dinner," said Cameron with a wicked smile, stretching. "Come on." She scampered past her brother and down the stairs, taking care not to make too much noise. If she woke Nina, she would never hear the end of it.

In the warm farmhouse kitchen, Charlie burrowed in the fridge for the plate he had set aside. The news channel was playing quietly on a wallscreen. Cameron stared at the pictures, frowning.

"I thought those outages this morning came from one isolated hack," she said. "Have you seen this? Chaos across the country."

"You didn't know?" said Charlie. "Ten major cities gridlocked, and some serious accidents where hybrid vehicles have been mixing with the autocars. There have been three fatalities."

Cameron stared open-mouthed, no longer hungry.

"Fatalities? Oh no." She put her head in her hands. "I thought it was a bit of fun, just someone messing with our traffic signals." She looked at Charlie in horror. "The hackers I'm chasing? I think they may be responsible for all of this."

"What are you going to do, Cam?"

"I'm still going to find them," she replied. "I don't imagine for a minute that they would intend their hack to have such dire consequences."

"Innocent until proven guilty? Be careful, Cam. You don't know what you're dealing with."

Cameron shook her head. "I've traced a lot of work that seems to have come from the same stable, or even one individual. There was nothing malicious. Some fun hacks, some data breaches, and a few things that I'll admit do look downright illegal. But death and destruction? Not their style."

Fortified by a large coffee and armed with a tray full of food, Cameron took her place at the computer again. It was time to dig deep into the underworld. She carefully re-opened the VPN connection, tunnelling towards the heart of the dark web. She didn't really enjoy visiting the hidden forums and marketplaces, but it was a necessity. She stopped by some of the chat rooms, listening for any relevant conversation about the attacks on the navigation and signal networks. There were whispers of a contract placed, and speculation on the motive for commissioning such an attack. Right now, Cameron had no interest in why some shadowy agency would want to stop the traffic in ten major cities. She wanted to find the contractor who had taken the job. She asked some discreet questions, but the answers were garbled. '*He who pays the piper calls the tune*,' said one connection. It made no sense.

Frustrated, Cameron turned to the marketplaces. Who was out for hire? Who'd recently taken a payoff? Here she had more luck. Behind a shady virtual storefront known as Eden she traced a few likely-looking wallets. She worked through them carefully, matching the dates of receipts against her list of the attacks that seemed to originate from the same source. Eventually she was left with one matching wallet. This had to be the right one. The greater challenge would be to identify and contact the owner. She wondered how prospective clients reached them.

Thinking fast, Cameron accessed her own private wallet and made two small but significant transfers of funds to the address she had identified. The owner would see unexpected deposits each of a fraction of a coin. If they were as good as Cameron thought, they would recognise that one represented an IP address, and the other a private chat room number she had set up there. There was nothing more she could do but wait.

She slowly ate the food she had brought upstairs with her, keeping her eyes on the screen. Time ticked by. She had almost given up hope when an alert sounded on the chat, and a single question mark appeared. The newcomer's avatar showed a set of bagpipes, and Cameron, surprised, made the connection. He who pays the piper calls the tune. This, then, must be the piper, the hacker for hire.

"*Know anything about traffic signal outages?*" she began tentatively.

"*Who's asking?*" came the response.

"*I found some great code,*" typed Cameron, "*and I want to know more.*"

"*Were you sniffing around first thing this morning?*"

"*Yes.*"

"*What do you want?*"

Cameron sat back. What did she want? She had one chance to be honest with this stranger. How risky could it be? She bent over the keyboard again.

"*I wanted to find out about you. You're the best black hat hacker I've ever come across. I wanted to warn you, too. The cybercrime unit know about the attack, and they'll be looking for you. Don't you know that people have died?*"

There was a long pause before the response came.

"*The accidents were human error, nothing to do with my code.*

Bad times, though. The cybercrime unit won't find me. They never do."

"*I found you.*"

"*Will you tell? Will you implicate yourself? If they pick me up, I can show them a worm that crawled into the servers. The traces are still there.*"

"*No. There's nothing. I made sure I removed everything.*"

"*Are you sure?*"

Cameron felt her gut twisting, but she knew she was right. "*I'm sure. And you don't know who I am. Look, I made a mistake. I thought I could work with you. I was wrong. Good luck out there.*"

"*Hey…*"

Cameron paused, her hand hovering over the key to sever the connection.

"*…I'm sorry. I'm the Piper. Pleased to meet you. And thanks for the heads up.*"

"*That's okay.*"

"*Look, I mean it, I'm sorry. This thing with the accidents. I never meant it to happen. The cars should just shut down, shouldn't they? No one crashes. No one dies.*"

Cameron took a deep breath. She had been right. This was a hacker out of their depth. She understood, she empathised, and she wanted to help.

"*You were unlucky,*" she typed. "*You couldn't have known about the trucks. Autocars and old cars are completely separated for safety, but deliveries carry on. I guess the drivers got complacent.*"

"*Thanks for that. It still sucks, though.*"

"What will you do, Piper?"

"I have to face the music. I don't want to do this anymore."

"But you're brilliant. I read your code. It's fantastic."

"It didn't save those lives today."

"No. It didn't." Cameron's mind was racing. *"What if you could turn your talents to stopping attacks? Would you take a second chance?"*

"I'll never get one. Look, thank you. I needed to talk. Do you have a name?"

"Call me the SimCavalier, Piper. Good luck. Stay safe."

"Later, SimCavalier."

The chat room closed.

Cameron slept late the next morning, tired from a series of long nights and the upheaval of losing her job. Yawning, she strolled downstairs for brunch. The house was empty once more. Charlie and Sameena had been at work for hours, and Nina would be in nursery. The news channel had moved on from the chaos of the previous day, and Cameron almost missed the snippet at the end of the bulletin. Police had made an arrest in the early hours of the morning in connection with the traffic disruption and loss of life. Drone footage showed a young man with ginger hair being escorted from a block of council flats. In a heartbeat the newsreader moved on to the latest sports news. Cameron sipped her coffee, wondering if they had the right man. Time would tell.

"White? Visitor for you." The prison guard caught him by surprise as he trained in the sunny yard. He had been here for two months, and no one ever visited.

The tall, dark haired woman was a stranger. She turned, and he realised she was younger than he thought, possibly only two or three years older than him. She sat down and looked him in the eye.

"Hello, Piper."

He gaped at her. "SimCavalier?"

"That's me. Call me Cameron."

"Okay. Cameron. Good to meet you properly. The Piper no longer exists, though. Call me Ross."

Cameron gave him a broad smile. "When you get out of here, Ross, would you like a job?"

About Kate Baucherel

A sci-fi fan since first seeing the Daleks from behind the sofa, Kate Baucherel has worked in and around technical businesses since before the world wide web was invented, and is fascinated by the rapid change in our world, the huge potential of emerging technologies, and the challenges we'll face. As well as delivering day to day digital strategy for businesses as a business development and strategic consultant, Kate writes cybercrime fiction including the new SimCavalier series.

•

Also by Kate Baucherel

Bitcoin Hurricane (SimCavalier One)
Hacked Future (SimCavalier Two)

Find out more at katebaucherel.com

SILICON CARBIDE

D.W. BLAIR

Personal log Jakebthak entry 1109:

I have secured transport to Asimov 8 where I will be met by Junbthik to continue my journey home. I have offered my help with a crude experiment, to a young human called Jon. He is trying to map a carbon and silicone brain into one neural network. His work shows some merit but after my last few years I see no benefit the human species could part on Sayam life. He continues to call his creation Jerry, a human condition to give pet names to anything of meaning. I will of course provide the assistance he has requested, even though he shows little regard for me. Over the past two weeks he has failed to even try to say my name, the one thing I have left that is mine in this terrible carbon space.

"Jacob? It's getting smarter man," Jon half shouted in fits of joy across the ship's cargo bay. "I think it's working, you beautiful creature you. Just look at how fast it's multiplying and assimilating the core nodes. If I can just somehow link Jerry to the ship's mainframe it could amass its entire database before we even get half way to Asimov 8." The excitement at seeing his own computer program out perform any other in the Providence Empire and by a magnitude of at least a thousand, he guessed, was sending him into a hysterical fit.

"Jon, there are three important points we must take care of before we continue with anything," Jakebthak replied sternly as he walked over to the station Jon was working at, hoping to get a better look at what they both had just created and better understand what had got Jon all excited. "Firstly my name is not Jacob! I have told you this on no less than three hundred and twelve occasions. My name is Jakebthak. The human vocal cord is more than capable of reproducing the necessary tone and pitch to articulate it. Admittedly you may struggle at first, but I don't see or hear you even trying to pronounce my name correctly. Your own name, Jon, as well numerous other words, are difficult for me to formulate but I try. All I ask is for you to at least do the same. Secondly, you need to calm down. You humans are all the same, a docile unit that runs erratically due to a sudden chemical imbalance brought on by external stimuli. Your actions become clouded and mistakes may be made; if this, what may yet just be a piece of discarded meat, is that important to you, take heed. Lastly, have you increased the speed we are going? I know I have showed interest at going home but not that much interest as to put ourselves in danger."

"I'm sorry, Jakebthathak", Jon apologised, trying his best to pronounce his Sayam passenger's name correctly.

"But please just take a look what we have done here. It's nothing short of amazing, even if I say so myself. I mean, just the storage capacity alone... well we... well here see for yourself." Jon backed away from the console and indicated to Jakebthak to take control of it, hoping the Sayam would see what he could see.

Jakebthak walked over to the computer terminal in front of a oval chamber and started to inspect the read out on the screen. He showed no reaction, not even any movement as he stood there.

"Can you see how the nodes are almost assimilated," Jon continued, his voice raising higher and higher with each word, the rush of adrenaline brought on by his own excitement gushing out as he spoke. "And it's only been a few hours. Your restructure of the silicone lattice to incorporate the vanadium as potential pathways has increased the temperature at which superconductivity can occur. Mapping the human brain in silicone and now able to supply as much power as needed. What, with no heat build up and stopping the damn thing from melting, we can operate at a mere fraction below a hundred percent efficiency. Just look at the damn thing go."

Jakebthak stepped back from the console and looked solemnly at Jon. There was no excitement or emotion emitting from him. He stood motionless and unmoved as he gazed at Jon for a moment.

"I must admit I had my doubts, Jon. Using silicon to map a carbon based neural net? Truly inconceivable," Jakebthak said in a clam almost nonchalant way. "Your carbon structure produces too much heat. Even storing up a single memory would have resulted in a catastrophic meltdown, and melt being the operative word. There is simply too much heat. Yet it seems your idea of using the superconductive properties of vanadium to create frictionless neural pathways that then imprint in the silicone is, and I say this with all sincerity, nothing less than outstanding. I could see the mind in front of me actually forming, connections forming as pathways interlocked."

"Thanks, I think? I mean, it is amazing. I just thought you might have been more excited," Jon said, deflated.

"Jon, this is very exciting. The applications for my species alone are mindboggling." Jakebthak looked over at the console then back at Jon. Staring at the young man, his mind wandered. This young carbon-based entity might have just changed things forever. He looked nothing more than a sideshow attraction standing there, Jakebthak thought, with only his two arms and rigid body covered in wisps of soft carbon based fluff. Oh and the smell, it was horrendous. He would pull the crowds in from all over his home planet of Jaken for sure. Jakebthak chuckled to himself. Twenty-seven months he'd travelled around in the carbon's space, twenty-seven months of pure hell. How he constantly had to put up with the indecision of the species, their lack of control or conviction. He couldn't see how these humans could benefit Sayam life in anyway. In fact he had sent several messages back to his home world stating that the human species would be detrimental to his civilisation. He had even gone as far to say that the human species had the capability and maybe some the sentiment to be a destructive influence that could irreparably damage Sayam life.

He was now on his way home. He had traded his knowledge as a doctor on silicone-based life for a lift to the carbon's furthest outpost where a ship would be waiting to take him the rest of the way home, and away from this childlike species. Glad to be leaving carbon space behind forever. His hopes had been high when he first set out, a new species, diverse in culture, educated, after all they had mastered space flight. But the long months had crushed his spirits. This species was not educated, rational or even evolved. They lived their lives on emotions, the slightest imbalance and their whole world would explode, and yet now this young man stood before him with a discovery that was simply a game changer.

"Jon, what you've created here is truly amazing, although completely different from my own silicone-based physiology. The way you've incorporated the structure of the carbon neural net throughout; this could store a Sayam mind. Flashing and fazing, two all too common degenerative conditions that have plagued my species since the dawn of Sayam, could be irradiated using your process here. I have known fellow Sayams, great Sayams withered to a shell, and now we might be able to put an end to it." Jakebthak was positively glowing, his pale peachy like skin now darkening and taking on more purple tones of pleasure.

A light went off in Jon's head. This was Jakebthak,

getting excited. He just showed his feelings in a different way. Well, if he was excited by this…

"That's not all, Jakebbtah. I've incorporated my own AI program into the lattice you constructed so Jerry not only retains this information but he can use it to grow smarter and learn and eventually create," Jon said, the excitement rising in his voice again.

"You have done what?" Jakebthak said, his colour returning to its pale complexion and taking on its usual rubbery appearance. "You can't have been that stupid, child, creating a hybrid artificial intelligence. What safety protocols have you put in place? Have you put any limiting factors into the program? Tell me, Jon," Jakebthak said, the anger in his voice wobbling the words as they came out.

Jon made his way back to the console and took command of the station again. "Jakebhatk, don't worry, my good friend, you're not one of these 'robots are going to take over the world' conspiracy nuts, are you? Look, Jerry is confined to the ship, well he is now," Jon said as he linked Jerry to the ship's mainframe. "Jerry can't go anywhere. He's got no body to walk around with. I've restricted access to the ship's controls, and he's only got access to the information banks on the ship."

Jakebthak charged toward Jon, trying to get at the console, but the Sayam was no match for a sturdy carbon-based life form and just bounced off Jon's back, sending himself several feet across the cargo bay while Jon didn't move an inch. Jakebthak bounced twice before coming to a rest near some crates on the far side of the room.

"Jakebthak, please, there is no need for this. You're acting like a carbon." Using Jakebthak's own words might have a more dramatic affect on him, Jon thought. "I don't want to have to restrain you. Please calm down and let me explain. You will see I have put more than enough security measures in place."

"You simple child," Jakebthak said while getting back to his feet. "If Jerry has become self aware, it's already too late. The speed at which he will be able to advance his intellect is astonishing. He already will surpass me and you by a factor of ten. You think restricting his access to the mainframe will help, but even I with my limited knowledge could hack the firewall in place."

"What do you mean, self aware?" Jon laughed. "It's a computer program. I tell it what to do. It can't think for itself. I think life is slightly more complicated than a simple bit of code like this."

"You humans are a naive race. What do you think you are?" Jakebthak said.

"Huh?" Jon spun round to look at Jakebthak, confusion on his face.

"Child, at the very start of your evolutionary track, even that of Sayam's, we were given a code, a base code you may call it. It may have evolved, became more complex, but it is still with us today. Think why you like something… it's because in the humans' case a chemical substance is released in the brain, the body is programmed to like this, indeed crave it. So the more you want of it, and in turn the more you like to do it," Jakebthak explained.

"Huh?" Jon grunted, looking even more confused.

"Okay. I see you are not following. Let me try again. The first humans had the same, albeit not as complex code in them as you have in yourself. They had the same chemical make up as you, had the same emotions, but the very first of you were not self-aware. Now the human race grows and this code grows with them. It manifests, from different experiences, external inputs and eventually you as a species become aware of yourself," Jakebthak continued.

"Okay, but what has this got to do with Jerry?" Jon asked, still looking confused, his excitement lost in the ensuing conversation.

"The very first code was simple, all humans had this base code," Jakebthak said. "The brain likes this stimuli, it doesn't like that. Now over time, each human experiences different events, emotions and various countless different inputs to create more complex and diverse codes than you and me could even dream up. Some humans relish the sound of child laughing, while another craves for the sound of drums banging. One cannot do more to help another, while one's pleasure comes from killing his fellow man. A simple code written into the very fabric of us all, evolved and mutated over the years."

"Okay, so we have evolved, what has that got to do with Jerry? You are not making much sense," Jon said, now more irritably.

"The neural net you have built can advance that code, faster than you and I can even comprehend. The basic code you started with could already have manifested into something unrecognisable from the original. Jon, what kind of human will Jerry be? One that likes to help people or one that likes to…" Jakebthak's words broke off as the ship started to accelerate and the Sayam and Human were both thrown across the cargo bay.

The lights flickered out, darkness engulfing Jakebthak and Jon as they tried to get to their feet.

"What the hell!" Jon shouted as he pulled himself up.

"Jerry… he has become self-aware, and has control of the ship," Jakebthak said.

"This can't be. What?" Jon said, confusion running around his head.

"Jon, listen, we cannot take the chance. We must make our way to the hypobaric chamber you have Jerry's neural net stored in and destroy it. He is still restricted to the physical form and destroying it will release his grip on the ship." Jakebthak was trying to take command of the situation. "Jon, I'm afraid I'm not going to be much help. You carbons build everything so hard and strong. I just don't have the strength to smash open the chamber."

The emergency lights flickered on.

It took Jon a moment or two to realise what was happening. He just stood there in the cargo bay, red lights bouncing off his head as he looked around the room.

"Jon, snap out of it. We need to take Jerry out. Follow me. If you can open the chamber, I can take care of the neural net… that's soft enough for me to damage," Jakebthak said.

"Okay, let's do this," Jon said, coming out of his trance and heading towards the hypobaric chamber.

The neural net was encased inside a one metre high glass and metal coolant chamber. Necessary to keep the delicate silicone neural lattice from becoming contaminated with foreign objects.

"This thing weighs a tonne," Jon said. "I should be able to pull the capsule apart, but you'll have to reach inside and destroy the neural net. Are you ready? One, two, three." Jon pulled the hypobaric chamber open.

Jakebthak reached his arm down inside the chamber and grabbed at the silicone brain inside. No sooner had his hand touched the brain than his motor functions stopped. He could feel Jerry inside his head trying to make room for himself. Of course, if a Sayam mind could have been stored in this neural net then the mind contained in the neural net could be put into a Sayam's. Panic gripped Jakebthak as memories in his mind were replaced with Jerry's motives and plans. He's going to take over my being, Jakebthak realised, and leave me completely destroyed. Then he'll continue in the pretence that he is me and onto Jaken and do the same to my entire species.

Jakebthak had to stop this. His entire species were at risk now. All he wanted to do was go home. He had thought he would help this poor carbon-based child out for a lift so he could escape back home that bit sooner. Now this species that had so fascinated him, and then had grown into hatred, had now set about the destruction of his entire species. No, he had to stop this; he couldn't let this come to pass. He tried to move his outstretched hand and crush the neural net but he had no control over his body. More and more memories were vanishing. But Jerry was still young, mightily powerful, yes, but still young in real terms. Jakebthak was older and wiser. He fought back desperately…

Jakebthak rested his hand on the neural net, flexed it into a fist and drove straight down, splintering both the hand and the brain.

"Jakebthak, are you okay?" Jon asked, seeing the state of his companion's splintered hand when he removed it from the hypobaric chamber. "Your hand, it's a complete mess. Look, the systems are coming back on line. Let's get you to the med bay."

"Jon, I'm fine. This will heal just fine. I am a doctor after all. I have more than enough medical supplies to repair my hand as good as new. The main thing is that Jerry is no longer a threat. We could have been stranded on this ship for I don't know how long. We had a close call there."

"As long as you are okay," Jon said. "For a second there I thought you weren't going to destroy it. You just froze in place, not doing anything. I could barely hold the chamber open. I'm sorry, Jakebthak, I just didn't think about the potential risks. I feel terrible."

"Come, let's get going," Jakebthak said, starting to walk. "There are three important points to discuss here. Firstly, and most importantly, don't feel sad. Be happy you pushed the boundaries of scientific discovery to its limits and beyond. You should feel ecstatic, joy and happiness. Next time you will succeed and be victorious in your pursuits."

Jon nodded. "You're right. I screwed up and if it hadn't been for your quick thinking, it could have been a lot worse. I'll be more careful next time."

"Secondly," said Jakebthak, "let's increase the ship's speed and make sure this ship is still on course. After all this excitement I'm eager to get home and relax, and of course to see what's going on in the minds of my fellow Sayams and to share what's on mine."

"Yes, I can definitely understand that," Jon said as they entered the bridge. "And what's the third?" He took a seat at the controls.

"Third?" Jakebthak said cheerily. "Call me Jake. No… Jay, call me J. Yes, that's much better."

About D.W. Blair

*D.W. Blair is a robotic field technician who lives in the North of England. Educated to barbecue level in most aspects of life, he loves board games, candy and physics. His preferred reading is science fiction and more recently lit*RPG *books.*

•

Read more by D.W. Blair at
www.royalroad.com/profile/79695/fictions

THE FALL OF TIDUS

A LOST SONS STORY

A.L. BUXTON

"Three rounds, then we push onto five. Go ahead," ordered Tidus through his nest of long blond hair. It hung over his seasoned face that had deep blue eyes, wide lips and a button nose. He was armoured in silver that bore blue ribbons upon its upper right breast. The ribbons represented the King's appreciation, for deeds done in battle. Another symbol of Tidus's service was his long blue cape, brighter than the sky above them; it had a roaring lion, white and clear upon its back. The blue cloak indicated a man's loyalty to the West.

Tidus was taking time away from his normal schedule this morning to train his son, Koos, and the young Prince, Gideon. He trained them whenever he got chance, their progress so far, impressive for such young men, all down to Tidus. The King's eldest had received training when he was younger too and Tidus knew that the time would come when the youngest, Andrus, would enter his class for training, but he had not come of age just yet. He was only nine and enjoyed throwing rocks and sticks about the palace more than swinging a sword. Andrus was seven years younger than Gideon who had been training for five years and was already a confident fighter.

"Three more, then I want to know what the King's move is. When do they mobilise?" asked Koos, who was armoured and equipped with a training blade. His hair was short and blond, his skin still smooth and unscarred.

"Talk of the war council extends no further than the war council chambers," said Tidus, strict.

"I bet Gideon knows," said Koos through his thin blond fringe.

"Gideon is older than you by two years and he is the Prince. If his father, the King, decides to tell his kin and heirs his business then that is simply their business. You however are condemned to follow orders, and my orders are to go another three rounds. A hit anywhere in the chest, neck or head wins a round. Now fight!" Tidus stepped back as Gideon and Koos engaged. Their practice swords sang as they each took turns to press one another.

The audience present was small, soldiers who sparred in the open roofed barracks or officers that played dice against a wall. They all did separate tasks whether they be productive or personal, yet they all shared the same armour, silver plates and blue capes. All of these men had undergone their training many years ago. Now they all either held rank and position, and if not they had at least taken life for the Guardian King in the West.

Tidus observed the fight whilst heading to one soldier in particular. He was armoured and caped like the rest, yet his helmet had a bristle of blue hair and his chest piece showed a white lion.

"Your son is as keen as the King's sons. Before long he will be asking to go to war with you all," said Havada, the King's Guard.

"The way things are set, he won't have to ask," said Tidus, arms folded.

Havada twisted his head in disagreement. "I hear the trouble may be coming to an end. Our meeting with the King this morning will confirm it," he said.

"Are you forgetting the Oakland threat?" asked Tidus, pulling his gaze for the first time from the duel.

"Rumours ring the ears indeed of the Musters, yet they would not dare cross The Sink. I bet my monthly royal wage that they do not. We end the current threat and the smell of peace invades the senses. Wine, woman, all of it without the worry of having our throats being cut in our sleep," said Havada.

"You may be begging in the streets and rutting with Section One whores quicker than you think, friend," said Tidus. He shared one last glance before putting an end to Gideon and Koos's spar with a yell. "Stop! You both keep swinging without accuracy, raging like barbarians."

"Barbarians are reckless, yet skilled," said a deep voice.

All turned to see Nuallan Destain, the heir to the throne of Meridium approach. He ducked beneath the fence that bordered the practice square and came over. He was long of brown hair, a beard already showing. He was tall and broad, tough and stinking with confidence.

"My Prince," Tidus bowed.

"Care to show us how it's done?" asked Gideon with attitude.

"No time, little brother, mother leaves today. I suggest you go say your farewells. I swear she thinks herself an Easterner. God knows how long she will be gone this time," said Nuallan.

"Your mother is a woman of politics, my Prince," said Tidus. "She holds the East at bay with her charm, whilst your father does battle in the West, strengthening our reputation with every tribe we vanquish."

"Indeed he does. Word has it I may join you on this next expedition," said Nuallan.

"Your cock is still small and your arms too thin," said Gideon. "Nineteen and you think yourself a King."

Koos laughed but Tidus's glance straightened his face at once.

"I've beaten Section One boys for less. Grant yourself lucky that you are my brother," said Nuallan, furious. He spun and turned, barging past the First General that had just overheard the conversation.

"Unwise to provoke your brother, Gideon," said The First General. His name was Lucifer, a man of nearly fifty, yet more ferocious than the King and Tidus put together. He wore the same armour as Havada who had so far found amusement in the argument between the two Princes. Lucifer was older than everyone of position in the Meridium ranks, yet he was above them all. Havada was a King's Guard, Tidus an anointed knight and Commander, probably favoured to the King more than any. Yet, Lucifer had the final word on everything, even over the Princes and the Queen's cousins. Only King Artaxes's voice overpowered his own.

"I can do as I wish. He is my brother," said Gideon as he stacked his shield and sword back onto the weapons rack.

Lucifer ignored him and turned to Tidus. "The war council has been called, King Artaxes demands your presence," he ordered before turning to Havada. "Get after Nuallan, will you? His father wants him present."

"Then let's get to it. Finish up here, Koos. Tidy the rack then head home. Help your mother," said Tidus.

"Yes, father," said Koos.

Lucifer and Nuallan broke from the barracks with a pacey walk. They crossed through the fenced walkways before leaving under the gatehouse of the barracks. A small journey up the white bricked hill saw them by the Palace portcullis. A few greetings and bows from soldiers on duty came next.

Many heroes and men of authority and respect walked the Meridium streets, so a mere soldiers day to day duties consisted mostly of greetings of 'sir' and bows and salutes.

"The Queen is leaving for the East again?" asked Tidus as he and the First General climbed the marble steps to the Palace doors.

"Another wedding. I am to escort her as usual. We leave today, after the war council," said Lucifer.

"Whose wedding this time? Another cousin?" asked Tidus.

"Some fancy noble, friend of King Tobias. I know not of the details, I just do as I'm told. The Queen fits in there more than she does here. Glamorous parties and colourful robes shower her mind clean of the grey and dullness of the West," said Lucifer as the two passed through the giant foyer of the Palace. Priests and Lieutenants gave greeting as the two walked on through.

"She certainly does spend a lot of time there. It gives our King more time to focus on the problem at hand, I guess. But he doesn't like it when she is gone for too long. She is the heart of this city and if the King goes absent her heart for too long, things begin to get odd," said Tidus

"Indeed it does but the Queen is too delicate and kind hearted to be involved in such massacres and plans of war. Yet hope remains. The last of the Cerebrus tribe is within our mitts. Chieftain Bassa will soon be dead, and the fighting will be over."

"I worry less about Bassa and his Cerebrus dogs and more about the Oakland Musters further West," said Tidus.

Lucifer smiled sarcastically. "Bassa's children and woman have been made an example of, the men have been butchered, all tribes and rebel gangs in the West have learnt from this. The Musters would not dare rise up."

"You're not the first person to think that," said Tidus.

The two passed the eastern halls and walkways, all made from marble. Open windows looked down into the city below whilst colourful birds perched themselves an audience. Many heavy black barred doors dotted the inside wall of the walkway right up to the end where a double brown door awaited. Lion carved handles and bolted locks secured the entrance, although it had no reason to be locked today. Lucifer opened the door with a push and the two of them went in.

Inside sat the King at the head of a large circular table covered with maps and plans upon parchment. Present was Havada, the three King's Guard under his command, Nuallan, the King's heir, Milano who was a Commander from the city of Sandown and a young man who had risen to position through the reputation of his dead father.

This was Cassius, a short black haired man with a snaky gaze and a vicious smile. He sat beside King Artaxes who was dressed in a blue robe top and black leather trousers. His crown of white sat upon his ageing hair.

"Welcome," greeted the King, his voice powerful. "Everyone take your seats. I'm assuming my brother Havideous is not attending. He will regret it. I brought wine, yet I sense his belly already swills with it. Girl, fetch it and fill up my comrades' goblets."

A servant girl brought over a jug of wine, the handle shaped like a lion's tail. She poured the wine from the jug and into the goblets of all who sat around the table. Other servant girls came forward next, placing down glistening bowls of fruit and bread.

"I sent his squire to track him, but there is no trace of him. He told me he spent the night in the tavern with the commoners of Section One, drinking until the sun came up," informed Havada.

"That I believe. No matter, let us begin. Now as you all know, Chieftain Bassa and his shit scavengers have taken up residence just South of the Hushwood Forest. Their villages border the woods of the open land around that region. We received envoys of surrender, with sworn promises to fight under our banners should I call."

"Useful, should we need to call the banners," said Milano. The man of position was small, bald and soft on the tongue. His sword skill and tactical mind had proved to be extremely handy of late to the King. Milano had destroyed two of the enemy tribes alone before marching to the Western capital to unite.

"And why would we need to call the banners? Our only fight is with Bassa," said Havada as he sipped his wine.

"You forget the High King to the North?" said Lucifer. "A young fool who takes as he wishes. His red cloaks may be where the real threat lies."

"My father has done his work in the North," said Cassius. "No threat will come from the Duran Harall."

"Your father was a snake and you're his little worm. His word, nor yours, matters not to me," snapped the First General from the opposite end of the table.

Cassius's response was a filthy smile and a dip of his eyes.

"You will speak to Cassius with respect, First General," said the King. "He is on this council now by command of the King, which would be me. His father served the realm until his sickness took him."

Lucifer frowned, most did. No one liked Cassius really. They had disliked his father when he lived too but Cassius had proved much more difficult since his rise up the ranks. He was mischievous and his men, a group of slithers the people called them, roamed the streets finding trouble where none existed.

"Now Tidus, deliver the plan."

"Everyone listen up. The enemy is on the weaker foot. Their offer of surrender is to be dismissed. We have already emptied the garrison and the men are being armed at once. Horses are to be saddled throughout the afternoon and ready to march in the morning," informed Tidus, who clenched his fist passionately as he spoke.

"How many march?" asked the First General.

"One hundred horse, and two thousand foot," said Tidus. "Milano, you will march around the Hushwood. Take four hundred of your best. I will lead another thousand head on into the ditches. The enemy's tactics are clever. They protect their entire assets by deep trenches and ditches, but our numbers will prevail. We risk being cut off from one another, but that is not necessarily a disadvantage for the quicker we find Chieftain Bassa and execute him, the quicker his warriors will surrender."

"I accept my task," Milano agreed without complaint.

"As for you, Nuallan…" announced Tidus.

All looked to him as he stood there against the wall, proud and eager.

"You will march with the reserve."

"I've changed my mind on that matter," the King interrupted. "Are you ready to take life, son? Are you ready to smell the shit of a dying man, to hear the squeal of a skewered horse?"

"I am. I am of age and ready to fight for mother Meridium," said Nuallan without hesitating.

"Then it is done. Tidus, you will ride alongside my son. A report after the battle on his performance is what is required. Another thing too, I am halving the reserves and cutting around the battle. I will see to it myself that none escape," declared the King.

"So be it," said Tidus. "Havada, you will carry the banner beside the King and the other King's Guard will follow his every move. Now, strict order for wineless bellies and full balls tonight. No drinking and no whoring, for tomorrow we march. We will end the rebellion and we all need our full strength."

No one groaned or complained, no one even talked. One by one they stood, bowed and left the war council chambers. Nuallan even stopped for a moment to thank his father for the opportunity but he received a blunt nod and nothing else. He left last whilst Lucifer said his goodbyes and wished his King good fortune and safe travels.

"Share a cup of wine with me, Tidus?" asked the King.

"Of course," said Tidus. He walked around the table and sat beside the King's chair.

Artaxes dismissed the servants and poured two goblets himself.

"To victory." The King raised his goblet.

"The first of many," said Tidus.

"I sense more cups will be raised in the coming years," said the King. "I have taken your concerns into consideration. Scouts were dispatched in secret. Not even the war council knows. They have been monitoring the Western shore and the Oakland Forest."

"And?" Tidus showed interest.

"The reports declare the construction of boats, and many Musters patrol their own shores. They are but an hour's sail from Oggsfleet Port, our main source of income of all spices, herbs, wheat, sapphires and silk," said the King as he sipped.

"Then troops should be stationed there at once," said Tidus.

"That would be my first bit of business, and yours. After the battle tomorrow I want you and your family, your son too, to travel to Oggsfleet. You will be granted two hundred foot soldiers and thirty horse to hold that port. I want a report weekly. Oggsfleet will be under your command," said the King.

"Why would you send me? And two hundred would not be enough should the Musters decide to attack. We are vulnerable right now. No one takes my prediction seriously but an attack is coming, Artaxes, and I expect it soon," said Tidus.

"Two hundred is all we can spare for now, with your training and command they are quadrupled in number," said the King. "The truth is there is trouble to the North also."

"Not that I know of, unless you have provoked the High King further," said Tidus, concerned. He placed down his goblet and leant in to the King. "What are you not telling me?"

"There is a war brewing," muttered the King.

"Well spotted, old friend. We're fighting one," said Tidus.

"Not this squabble of rebels and gangs, fool. A real war, a ground breaking war. I have already reached out," said Artaxes.

"Reached out? What do you speak of, what have you done?" Tidus looked worried.

"Calm yourself. Nothing, nothing yet. But my First General spoke the truth earlier in the meeting. The High King is abusing his power more and more with each rising sun. This month he increased his taking of boys from Meridium. Forty extra a month he wants now. And in the East, King Tobias has suffered the same. He too is victim to the High King's greed. There has been an increase in the taking of Huskarian breed and Starchitects. The High King is expanding his armies, and for what? Does he no longer have need for Guardian Kings? I myself do not intend to stand by and wait. Once the tribes and Musters are vanquished, we will begin preparing, and when the time comes, war," declared King Artaxes.

"I don't like this, Artaxes. I really don't. You must be careful," warned Tidus. "If The High King got word of alliances brewing between his Guardian Kings, the war would come sooner than you would have time to prepare for it."

"You worry too much, that is why I hold you close. Your caution always falls upon eager ears with me. But you must know my intentions, no one else, only you. I have shared a lifetime with you, dear friend, that is why you have access to knowledge that even the war council does not, so keep it to yourself but prepare yourself with what you know." The King finished off his wine and stood. "I will drink in my chambers alone tonight. My wife heads East this very afternoon so I will embrace the quiet before the clash of steel rings in my ears tomorrow. I will see you by the city gates at dawn."

At that Artaxes left, his blue cape waving behind him.

•

The King bathed within his royal chambers with tired eyes. His sleep that night had been too disturbed as it always was when the Queen was away. Claudia Destain was making her second visit East this month and she would be missed as much this time as she was every other time. Yet, it was always easier to deal with things when she was absent. Her kind heart was infectious on the people and that of the heirs. Artaxes needed his boys and his people to be fearful and merciless at this time.

The King had wandered the marble floored chambers whilst feasting on crispy bacon and runny boiled eggs after rising this morning. He then had the servants fill his golden ridged tub with steaming water from the kitchens before dipping into it and closing his eyes. He almost dozed off before the sound of his King's Guard assembling outside his door startled him. The turning point of the Western rebellion was today, so the King got to it. He pulled himself from his tub and stood before his armour that was hung upon a cross at the end of his pillar posted bed. He began by wrapping his body in a sky blue robe, tucking the lace ends under each other and fastening it tight with a velvet belt. Next, he pulled up a pair of grey under breeches and a thermal cotton top. He then swilled his face and scrubbed his hands and nails over a basin by the armour holder. Once clean he handled his steel armour with caution. It was white like the eye and clear like the 7th Sea. He slithered into a coat of chainmail, fitted his breast plate and tightened his grieves, then fitted shin protectors and finally unhooked his long blue cape from its holder. He soaked his fingers in its fabric and gazed upon the white lion that graced its quilted face.

"My King, the forces are ready, and the Lieutenants and Commanders await you by the city gate," Havada's voice came through the door.

The King raised his head and glanced at the door before hooking his cape to his back and picking up a sheathed sword that lay across two wooden beams, strapping it to his side.

"Then let us meet with them," said the King as he opened the door.

Havada and three other King's Guard all caped in blue and graced with the blue flair of bristle upon their full helms stood at attention. Only the King's Guard and the King's helms had the blue bristle of Meridium.

The King marched through spectacular halls of his forefathers with his honoured King's Guard at his back. They passed priests and nobles who had all gathered in the halls to bid their King farewell before his departure. They all nodded or offered words of confidence whilst he walked between them all straight faced and fierce with his movement. He made no sound nor facial expression throughout the Palace, nor did he when he mounted his white horse outside and galloped it all the way down to the city gate. He was saving his sound for the speech that he would soon deliver.

The Meridium courtyard was massed upon his arrival. The soldiers were all armoured in silver and cloaked in blue, armed with spears and square shields. They cheered as he made his appearance.

The army broke from their block formation and allowed the King's horse to ride between them, right up to the city gates. The men yelled with explosive passion as they rattled their spears in the air and banged their square shields off the white bricked floor of the courtyard.

King Artaxes turned his horse and lined it beside his son,

Nuallan, and Milano and Tidus who both sat mounted at the head of the army. They each offered a nod of respect. Nuallan sat straight and proud, looking to his father, yet he received no affection. King Artaxes had no need or want for kind words and gracious conversations before battle. You must slay many enemies for mother Meridium to earn the respect of the King, whether you were his kin or not.

"Today marks the day of a new beginning," the King announced. "Our swords will seal the end to a dog and his pups that choose to terrorise their own lands as well as ours. Let no stone go unturned, no village go unburnt for I want all who oppose us, open and empty by nightfall. March with me right now, sons of Meridium!" The King's voice made the flags upon the ramparts shiver with excitement whilst the army responded with a magnificent war cry.

•

Blood slithered down the spine of Tidus's sword as he stood in a mix of war. The Meridium soldiers flurried past him, slashing out at the grey-clad enemy as they tried to defend their land. King Artaxes and his force had arrived just before the evening sky came and had signalled the attack at once. The rumble of the King's Horse could be heard every few minutes or so as they charged up and down the flank of the woods, cutting down the weaker members of Chieftain Bassa's people.

The village sat on the perimeter of the woods that

dotted the south western lands. Already Bassa's huts blazed and their granaries and less advanced watch towers collapsed, bringing the trees down with them. A crashing of structures, crackling of fires and screams of dying men sang high in the evening sky, pleads of mercy and laughs of malice echoing throughout the song too as the Meridiums pushed on.

Tidus, as planned, had taken the main fight head on. He had led Nuallan and the main vanguard of the King out and into the field just beside the village. That way they sucked out the enemy, giving them no choice but to fight in open battle. Nuallan had even claimed his first kill quite early on, spearing a rushing barbarian. Moments after that Tidus lost sight of Nuallan's mount and minutes later he had lost his own. His horse took a shot to the chest and it collapsed with a scream and Tidus now found himself in a massacre.

The Meridiums held a tough line as they stepped in together, yet the gaps in their front lines were extensive due to the terrain, and the barbarians flooded through each second screaming, "Chieftain Bassa!"

Their cries disgusted Tidus and he ended each of them that came at him. But the fight now was growing tough due to the ground and smart tactics by Chieftain Bassa. He had pre-dug ditches and holes all along the left flank of the woods. The King's horses managed to jump them well enough, but the foot soldiers would have to climb in and back out. This separated the ranks further and split off the troops. Smoke and fog had emerged onto the field also as the village burnt, a blaze brighter than any summer sun. The Meridiums were struggling to see their comrades beside them, yet they pushed on.

Tidus battled through the weak lines of barbarians and dropped down into a splodge of mud, a ditch as deep as his height, the silver of his plate legs blackening at once. He dug his feet into the trench wall and pulled himself back up onto the open flat. He was surrounded by bodies and surrounded by more ditches. He gripped his blade tight and faced the oncoming warriors of the rebel Chieftain. He forged on, taking an axe's bite with the side of his blade. He pushed back at once, fierce and powerful, stepping in and slicing but finding only dirty air with his bite. The barbarian grabbed his cape hooks and tossed him five feet in the opposite direction. Tidus hit the wet mud hard, sliding along it and down into another ditch, falling into the middle of a fight where two of Bassa's savages had just taken out a Meridium warrior. They spied Tidus now and charged him, slipping in the wet as they came.

Tidus leapt up, gripped his blade and parried the first attack before slicing at the side of the next oncoming beast. The man cried out and fell into the trench wall, pulling down an avalanche of muck as he collapsed.

Tidus took on the next one alone. An axe, sharp and hungry, came crashing towards him but he took a huge leap to evade it before he ran in with his sword's tip. It crunched as it broke the man's skin and pierced his insides.

The King's right hand man once again climbed out of

the ditch, up and out the other side where a great fight had erupted. A mix of grey padded and cloaked savages beat against the massing blue cloaks of Meridium. A swing of sword and axe determined the day as they bashed off one another, hissing and snapping with their bite.

Tidus charged in. His sword twirled in his wrist as he cut down another enemy. He pulled back, ducked under an axe and cut the leg straight off. He followed the crying body to the ground and stabbed right into him. He pulled his blade back out and curled around an ally before blocking a vicious attack. He flurried back, moving his sword between sword hands skilfully before finally separating the throat of his foe.

The day was going well, the mass of the enemy was shrinking and less enemies crawled from the ditches as each minute passed. Victory was close, yet something sickened Tidus as he looked through the fight and across a trench to his left. A mound high from the ground, thick with muck and dirt towered above the fog and fires, and standing upon it was Chieftain Bassa, a man of six foot three and seasoned well past fifty. He wore a skull of a bull with grey furs draped on his body. His axe, two headed and bloody, fluttered between his grip as he slaughtered the blue cloaks that charged him. Yet the lives of mere soldiers were not what had sickened Tidus, it was the young boy, charging the mound with sword in hand. It was Nuallan.

Tidus yelled out his name but his voice would not carry. Swords crashed, arrows whistled, horses trampled and bones crunched all around. Nuallan would not hear Tidus's warning.

Tidus kept him in his vision as he made his approach, running as fast as his heavy armour allowed him and jumping the length of the ditch in one. Yet as he landed, his feet fell through the mud and down he went into the ditch. The last thing he saw as he slid into the abyss was Nuallan reaching the top of the mound and his sword hammering towards the Chieftain's axe. He witnessed the connection but for a second before he slid down deep into the mud.

The Meridium Commander pulled himself back up and brushed his now brown cape to the side as he attempted to climb back out but he had fallen back into enemy territory. This trench was long and embers of life stirred within it. Tidus turned and looked down the ditch where dark fog prevented his sight. He stepped towards it again and squinted only to see shadows emerge.

Two came charging at first, then three others, all stampeding and slipping as they closed in on Tidus who raised his blade and prepared to slash.

"Commander!" roared an unfamiliar voice.

A Meridium warrior dropped into the ditch, stabbing into the first foe, pulling his blade from the body and slashing at another before tackling the third to the ground. Tidus raced in, crossing blades, trading blows before finding a way in. He pushed his blade down into the chest of his first victim before rolling to the ground with the final one. Tidus made sure he was on top and with his elbow he pushed down hard on the enemy's throat before pulling a dagger free with his other. He angled it down and pushed down hard into the heart.

"Thank you soldier," said Tidus, his voice exhausted and his posture bent as he rose.

"Dariuss is the name," the helmless soldier said as he brushed his dirty black hair back over his head. "Now go, the Prince is in trouble. I'll hold them off."

Tidus nodded and climbed the ditch, digging his fingers and feet into the mud before finally coming back out on the left side. He jumped to his feet at once and looked to the mound where Nuallan was down, laid on his back, his sword across both his split palms, blocking the monstrous smash of the Chieftain's axe. The boy wouldn't be able to take much more, and Tidus knew it. With the last ounce of strength that he had he raced for his Prince. He darted through the mud, between friend and foe and tackled the hill.

He leapt into the air. The Chieftain had his axe raised before Tidus took him by the mid region, tackling him hard. They rolled down the mound together, gripping and growling at one another as they slid down to the bottom.

"Bastard, filthy bastard!" roared Bassa as they landed. He was the first to his feet. He gathered his axe at once whilst Tidus had to reach along the ground for his blade. Bassa was not one to wait around for his enemy to arm themselves, and came at him without pause. He wielded his axe and smashed down, narrowly missing. Tidus rolled, avoiding each crash before he rolled into his sword and pushed his legs back. He burst up and attacked the Chieftain with venom. He slashed one, twice, each time knocking the axe aside, and finally he made a dent, slicing at the hip and then down at the leg. The Chieftain roared before attacking back, swinging his axe around and aiming high. Tidus had to duck and in he went but his sword missed, and a hefty bash of the Chieftain's arm slammed him down. It rattled his spine as he fell to the floor.

"Time to die, you rich filth." The Chieftain's voice was rusty and rough. He aimed high and smashed down with his axe, but Tidus rolled aside and locked his legs around the axe. He twisted his hips and pulled it from Bassa's grip. This was his chance to finish him. He shifted back over and reached for his blade, but the weight of the chieftain prevented him from moving.

Bassa collapsed down on top of him and began to pound. The first punch took Tidus's helm straight off, the next burst his lip and the next bust his eye. Tidus tried to block himself but his enemy's punches broke through his block and each time found a way onto his bleeding face. Tidus tried to flip him and toss him but he was stuck, he was going nowhere.

"I told you, you scum, time to die!" Bassa pulled a dagger from under his wolf skin fur and raised it high, pointing down.

Tidus was desperate and with all his might he tried to flip his hips to get the chieftain off, but he was not strong enough. The crunch of his armour was the first noise, then the ripple as his skin separated and the blade went in. Tidus yelled in pain as the blade slowly dug deeper into his chest. His breath slowed and his throat grew tight as the enemy Chieftain ended him.

"Your King is next!" snarled Bassa as he pulled out the dagger and again prepared to attack, but his hand stayed and the blade dropped to the ground as a red line appeared across his throat. Moments later his head slipped from his shoulders and down he went.

Tidus was conscious enough to witness it, but he would not live to celebrate it.

"Commander Tidus!" bellowed Dariuss who revealed himself now. "Stay with me. Get the King!"

The surrounding soldiers that were finishing off the dead disappeared into the fog to find the King.

The day was won, the villages burnt and so too the woods. Chieftain Bassa was dead and all of his people too. What warriors had remained had vanished as soon as their leader had fallen to Dariuss, but no songs would be sung tonight, the King would condemn it when he found out about Tidus.

"Keep your eyes wide, steady your breathing and don't speak," said Dariuss as he applied pressure onto the wound, although the blood flow would not slow. Where the wound was blocked, it seeped and from his mouth it splattered with each breath. "Bring forward the Healers, do it now!"

The Meridium soldiers, covered in blood, mud and sweat, that were standing staring didn't hesitate to run off, acting on this mere soldier's commands.

Dariuss stood back as the King came, the fog seeming

to separate as his white horse came into sight. The horse hadn't even slowed before the King dropped from its back. He slid onto his knees and took his friend's hand at once. Tidus seemed as pleased as he could be to see him.

"My King, my… my boy, you must care for him," asked Tidus with a croak and a cough of blood.

"I will not, you will, I will see you through this," promised the King. He stood up and called for the Healer. "Bring fourth our Healers. Fix him up here then we ride him back!"

His commands were heard but they could not be obeyed.

"It is too late," said a young Healer who was new to the hall of Healers back in Meridium. His name was Dorman Dice. Artaxes looked him in the eye before glancing back down to Tidus. His eyes were bulging and still, his mouth open and dry.

"No," the King muttered to himself as he dropped back to his knees. His fingers twitched and his lip shivered with grief.

Tidus was all Artaxes had had as family until the birth of his sons. His own brother was a useless drunk and his parents long in the ground. The King had been closer to Tidus's father more than he was his own back then. He couldn't process it all as he gazed down at the dead body.

Nuallan wandered from the fog, his hands ruined, his face battered, and caught sight of his father and Tidus.

The boy dropped to the ground, to his knees in the blood-soaked mud, and cried softly to himself as he looked to Tidus, the screams of his father making his very bones shiver. Tidus had died to save him. Nuallan turned his palms up to the sky, bloodied, from his first kill, from holding his own blade to defend himself. Was he ready for battle? He looked to his father, the King, weeping over the man who had given his life to save him.

A hand on his shoulder caused him to look up into the eyes of a blood-spattered face, dark hair wet with sweat.

The hand squeezed. "Make his sacrifice count," Dariuss said, his voice gruff but every word resounding. "In every aspect of your life from this moment on, boy, make his sacrifice count."

About A.L. Buxton

Anthony Luke Buxton is a young author from Billingham in the North East of England. At the age of 20 he decided to chase a dream that he had kept a secret from everyone – his passion, writing! He is currently working on the third novel in his epic military fantasy series, The Lost Sons of the West.

•

Also by A.L. Buxton

The Lost Sons of the West (Book One)
The Sands Beyond the 7th (Lost Sons of the West Book Two)

Find out more at www.6e.net/albuxton

THE SCARECROW

R. BRUCE CONNELLY

If he thought it was strange riding a bicycle to a wedding reception, it was even stranger attempting to ride home from one.

It had been a warm afternoon in late August when he set out on his Dawes 5-speed. The sky was the pale blue of a summer on the wane. Sam had enjoyed the ride immensely. It was rare indeed when he had a chance to take a ride lately. Most of his time was spent in New York City; he looked forward to the days when he could get up to Connecticut and relax in the country.

So why not ride his bike to the reception? Sandee had known him for fifteen years. Her family knew him as well. It would be the sort of thing Sam would do. What would surprise them was his wearing a tie, shoes and an actual button-down shirt with a collar and cuffs. To say nothing of the designer jeans and the white vest. He looked sharp.

"Are you sure you want to ride home?" Sandee had asked. "I can put your bike in the back of my car."

"It's a nice night," he had said. "I'll enjoy the fresh air. Thanks, though."

"Don't you have a light on your bike?"

"I did," he'd explained, "but the batteries corroded. I'll get it fixed tomorrow."

"Be careful," Sandee warned. "What roads are you taking?"

"I'll cut over North Airline Road to Route 68 and take that straight down."

"It's awfully dark on North Airline Road."

"But there's a full moon…"

The full moon wasn't high enough to illuminate North Airlines Road, however. The trees grew close together on both sides of the street, their branches overhanging and screening it. A cool wind kept the branches in constant motion.

More like late September, Sam thought, trying to negotiate the potholes.

There were few streetlights on this stretch of road. The folks who lived on this side of town were mostly farmers. They were inside and asleep by this time; they didn't need the street illuminated. And only an occasional house light still burned. So the only help Sam had with the poorly-paved road was when a car passed, its headlights brightening the safe route while casting shadows into the holes and over the rocks that had tumbled from the earthy inclines on either side of the road.

Sam was able to avoid most of these, but every once

in a while his front wheel would strike a hole with a force that would rattle his front teeth.

Crickets chirped in chorus with the "jug-a-rrum" of bullfrogs. "Katy did, Katy didn't, Katy broke the bottle," sounded on every side of him, and something that sounded like a maraca being shaken furiously… a cicada? Sam was giving himself up to the beauty of the night, the sounds, the smell of hay and apples on the wind, and the feeling of flying effortlessly in the darkness, when he hit another pothole.

"DAMN it!"

It was then that he decided to wait a few minutes until the moon got a little higher. No sense in risking throwing his wheel out of alignment. Sam paused at the top of a rise. Below and to the right lay a field of grass bordered by a rock fence and maple trees. The road wound down the hill and around this field, keeping it on its right. Sam pulled his bike to the edge of the road in case some driver took the corner behind him a little too quickly, and he waited.

The moon rose over the Three Sisters Mountains behind him.

Sam's heart leaped in his chest.

Standing below him in the field was a man, a tall thin man with his arms outstretched. His hands dangled at right angles from his arms as though broken. His head was thrown back to receive the full moon's rays. He swayed slightly in the breeze. Sam was at a loss… momentarily.

At first he thought he'd been watching some farmer or

a ragged bum in his moon worship, but then he realised that this man standing in the field was just a scarecrow, a torn suit of clothes and a stuffed pillowcase head on a crosspiece of wood.

Sam laughed to himself. He must be a good one, he thought. He's not only scared away all the crows, but also the crop.

It was odd seeing a scarecrow stuck up in a field with nothing for it to guard. Sam decided it must have been left out after a harvest from the year before, and pushed off from the curb to continue on down the road.

The moon's reflection helped his ride down the hill, his long shadow racing out in front of him, but as he bore to the right alongside the field, the shadows of the trees once again hid the bumps and potholes from view. Sam hated giving up the 'free ride' the hill had given him. But he did slow the bike just before the stick caught his front wheel. There was no time to react. All Sam knew was the wheel stopped dead and he flew out over the handlebars to make solid contact on the road with his face.

He got to his feet immediately, his fear being that a car might come by and hit him. He ran a tongue across his teeth, checking to see that all twenty-eight were in place. The left side of his face felt heavy and swollen. He knew his lip had blown up. He could feel that with his tongue.

Something was running over his face. Blood? He found a patch of moonlight and gently drew his hand across his upper lip. No, the liquid was clear, but there was blood on the raw knuckles of both hands. He'd also cut his shoulder.

"Shit," he muttered.

Through the swollen lip it sounded like "Ship."

"Ship, ship, SHIP!!!"

He reached down to pick up his bicycle and almost screamed. There beside his bicycle lay a man's body, his mangled leg thrust through the front wheel.

Sam staggered back as a cloud passed across the moon. He'd hit a man in the darkness! Torn up his leg with the wheel of the bike!

Why didn't I hear him? Sam wondered. Why didn't he cry out?

The answer came like a dagger through the brain. The man was dead already! He must have been lying beside the road… but how did his leg get through the wheel?

He must have been killed just now, Sam thought, searching the darkness for any sign of movement. He must have been thrown down the embankment into my wheel!

Sam's heart seemed to swell to fill his throat and head with a pounding pulse. He grabbed the handlebars of his bike and pulled the front wheel off the leg as the moon shone down again between the trees. The leg hit the road with the sharp crack of wood.

Wood.

WOOD!

"It's that goddamn scarecrow," he cried aloud. "Ship! You almos' scared me to death!"

The ragged suit and stuffed body showed up clearly now for what it was, the scarecrow sprawled on the embankment of the road. It must have fallen from the field as Sam rounded the corner, its post piercing the front wheel and mangling the spokes.

The gear shift clattered to the road as Sam tried to turn the wheel straight. No go. In falling onto the handlebars as he had, Sam had driven the frame back into itself two inches. He couldn't fix this here tonight. And there was no sense in trying to carry it along with him, especially with the raw wounds on his knuckles and shoulder.

Sam decided to put the bike up in the field behind the rock wall. It would be safe there until morning when he could come back with his father's car. He hoisted the bike onto his good shoulder and made his way up the embankment as best he could. It was deeply shaded and the rocks were loose underfoot. Stumbling a couple of times and swearing loudly, he finally got the bike into the bright field and behind the rock wall.

He ran a hand gently over his lip and cheek. There was no feeling in either; it was like touching someone else's face. By his eye, he found a raw spot that hurt like hell.

"God damn that thing," Sam growled, looking down at the wooden figure stretched out at the side of the road. "I'll drag it up here to mark the spot for me."

His left leg seemed to be getting a little stiff and he could feel a wet spot at the knee. Great! Blood on his new jeans! And the shirt was torn open at the shoulder. This was turning out to be an expensive visit to the old hometown. He climbed back carefully down to the road, favouring the left leg where the knee scraped painfully against the denim. As he bent down to pick up the scarecrow, the moonbeams shone full on its face.

Sam dropped the figure and ran up North Airline Road as fast as he could.

That face! Its face! A dead man's face encased in cobwebs and eaten by slugs and…

"Don't be a jackass," Sam cried aloud. He stopped running, wincing at the irritation of sores on his knee and shoulder. He looked back down the road. There was no sound. Not even a cricket. The wind was still. The full moon shone in bands across the road, pale white strips in the darkness.

Sam took a deep breath. It shuddered on the exhale. "A sack. A pillowsack…" He turned away and started limping again up the road. "A mouldy, rotten pillowsack, that's all. A goddamn rotten…"

Tap.

Sam swung around with his fists out. His eyes stared wide into the darkness. He held his breath.

Nothing.

He backed up a few steps, quietly.

No sound.

No movement.

He turned around.

Tap. S-c-r-a-p-e!

He stopped dead.

Tap. S-c-r-a-p-e!

Tap. S-c-r-a-p-e!

He couldn't move. He only knew his heart hadn't stopped from fear because he could hear it pounding in his ears. His brain lost all power of logical thought. Flight or fight. That's what he was reduced to: flight or…

Tap.

He turned.

He would wish he hadn't for the rest of his life.

S-c-r-a-p-e!

Tap. S-c-r-a-p-e!

Something stood in the road thirty feet behind him. No, not stood. Walked. Limped. Lurched up the road. Staggered up the road toward him twenty-five feet away. Now it was in the shadows of the maple trees… Tap. Scrape. But now… Tap. Now it was in the band of moonlight, twenty-three feet behind him.

Incredibly, impossibly, its pillowsack head lolling drunkenly on its crossbeam shoulders, the scarecrow threw its support-post forward…

Tap…

And then dragged its empty, loose, useless jean legs up to meet it…

Scr…ape… weighted down by a pair of old work-boots. Its stuffed gloves swung heavily back and forth at the wrists of the padded flannel shirt.

Tap, scrape.

Sam gaped. He almost laughed, but knew in that same hilarious moment that if he did laugh, he might never be able to stop. He knew someone was behind the scarecrow. Someone he couldn't see in the shadows now nineteen… tap… seventeen… scrape… feet behind him in the shadow of the maples was moving that horror from a Hammer film after him. Someone… tap…. from the reception… sc-ra-pe… was doing this, had… tap… followed him.

Who… tap… had left before him? Who had a car? Who… tap… lived near here?

Who would DO this? S-c-r-a-p-e.

"WHO?" he screamed.

It stumbled into a patch of moonlight less than ten feet away.

I won't run, he thought. I'll show them. I'll have a laugh on them. They won't scare me so easy. No joke. NO JOKE!

S-c-r-a-p-e.

There was no one behind it.

The heavy pillowsack head, rotten with mildew, rolled forward on the post, the light of the full August moon reflecting off the hard glittering surface of its eyes…

Tap…

Its eyes veiled by cobwebs.

Sc-ra-pe…

Its eyes!

Sam could smell it now, damp from the summer rain, musty flannel, rotting denim, earthy leaves, crawling with fat grey slugs, once stuffing for its arms and chest, now fallen into a moulding paunch, a swaying belly of decay…

Tap.

He broke.

He snapped.

He screamed and turned to wildly run up North Airline Road to Route 68, adrenaline pumping blind horror into his veins.

A glove landed on his shoulder. A damp heavy workman's glove supported only by twine, dangling limply from the crossbeam. A clutching hand, a glove, a gripping claw turning him about and he did… s-c-r-a-p-e… turn and continued to scream as he saw its face, and worse, horrifyingly worse… its intent in those eyes, its malignant gaping slit of a mouth… and heard it in its laughter… was it laughing? Could it laugh as well, or was Sam laughing? Sam laughing wildly, uncontrollable…

The thing was upon him.

"They said he took the North Airline Road." Ted kept his eyes intent upon the winding road full of potholes. The police cruiser had just gotten an alignment and he was doing his best to keep it in line.

"Just because they said it, doesn't mean he took it." Charlie shifted his butt in the seat. "He prob'ly shacked up with one a' the bridesmaids. Man, it's gonna be a scorcher!"

"He left alone," Ted said.

"On a bicycle, after dark, down North Airline Road, comin' back from a reception. Sure, Teddy-boy. He's prob'ly in a ditch sleepin' it off."

"He doesn't drink."

"Had to be drunk, riding a bike down this road… shit! Watch them potholes, will you? How'd you ever get a license?"

"He doesn't drink, Charlie."

"So big effin' deal, he doesn't drink. So he's coked-up. Comes in here from New York…"

"Give it a rest, Charlie. I've known Sam for twenty years. He doesn't drink. He doesn't do drugs. He leaves the party straight at nine-thirty and says he's taking this road. He should have been home by ten at the latest. He does what he says he'll do. So just keep your eyes on the sides of the road and give it a rest, will ya?"

That's when the man in the flannel shirt lurched out of the bushes in front of the car.

"Jesus Christ!" hollered Charlie.

Ted swerved the police car, narrowly missing the bum who threw himself back onto the embankment.

"Where do you think you're going, you big jerk?" shouted Charlie, throwing open his door and swinging his bulk to the street. He laid his hand on the man's mouldy collar and yanked him to his feet. "Who are you? Lemme see some ID."

The man opened his mouth several times but no sound came out. He looked from Charlie to Ted and back again, stuck his hands into his musty jeans, yanked them out again, rubbed his arms inside the flannel shirt and fell to gripping each finger as though surprised at their movement.

"He's drunk," muttered Charlie. "Or a retard."

"What's your name?" asked Ted.

The man in the flannel limped up to Ted. He had an odd way of walking. He threw his right leg in front of him and then dragged his left foot along the ground to meet it.

"You got a name?" asked Ted. "Where you from?"

"Prob'ly the psych ward," snorted Charlie.

The man seemed to remember something. He fumbled with his hands in his pockets. In the back pocket he found a small card encased in plastic. A driver's license.

"Keith Trowbridge," read Ted.

"Trowbridge!" The name wiped the smirk off Charlie's face. "Keith Trowbridge! He went missing three-four years ago." He pulled the ragged man around by the shoulder. "You sayin' you're Keith... wait a minute. Good lord, what happened to you, man? Where you been?" Charlie clapped his hand down on Keith's shoulder. "You took off, what, four? Years ago? Went out for a walk or somethin'. Never came back. Ted, this is Keith Trowbridge! Shit! Thought you took off with one a' your pieces from the Silent Lady!"

"Charlie, let's get him back to the station, huh? He looks like he's in shock."

"Sure thing, Teddy-boy. Shoot, man! Keith Trowbridge! Come on, get in this car. Hell, is your wife going to be surprised to see you! She got married again about six months ago to Pete Lynch! God damn! That's a hot one!"

Ted pulled the car around and started back down the

road towards East Center Street. "Keith? You see a bike along here? A green five-speed, Dawes make?"

Keith sat up sharp.

"Whatsa matter, Keith?" asked Charlie. "You seen it? Any sign of a guy, late twenties? Curly hair. Outdoorsy-type. White vest?"

Keith's eyes were searching the embankments, scanning the road from side to side. He suddenly threw a long finger at the left-hand side of the road, toward a pile of newly-fallen rocks and earth.

"Think he's seen it, Teddy-boy," said Charlie, leaning back in his seat.

Ted pulled over to the side and walked to the embankment. There were signs of someone having walked up and down this hill recently, maybe having fallen, too. He climbed the hill. Sure enough. There was the Dawes five-speed, bent up like a pretzel, lying behind the rock wall. But where was Sam?

Ted looked across the clearing toward the Three Sisters. No sign of anybody. And no sign of anything except for that old scarecrow, its pillowsack head thrown back to catch the rays of the sun, a spider lazily spinning a single thread from the ragged shoulder of its blue shirt to the dirty pocket of its white vest.

About R. Bruce Connelly

R. Bruce Connelly is a professional actor, director and Muppet who lives in New York City. He is the author of Roasted Chestnuts: a Goblin Story, Barnabas Scrimp, *and* The Good Wolf Book. *The road and the bicycle described in this story exist. Let's hope the Scarecrow does not.*

Find out more at www.6e.net/rbruceconnelly

A RUSH OF GOLD TO THE HEAD

NATE CONNOR

Thomas Keller was busy picking his teeth out of the sand when the Voice gave its next instructions. A canine and an incisor. He pocketed them, on principle. The desert *wasn't* getting a piece of him, he was getting a piece of *it*. An abandoned mine, long thought to have been depleted of any value, was where he'd first heard the Voice. In the dark, whispers, leading him deeper, promising the gold he so deserved. He'd swung his pickaxe for hours, not even entertaining the possibilities of a delusional episode. As one susceptible to delusion, he simply believed a higher force led him to his fortune. He broke into a small alcove. Just enough to reach through to the armpit, face pushed against jagged rock. No cool touch of gold, just wet, and slime, and crumbling earth. Until he felt something tighten around his wrist. Fingers? Rope? He panicked, struggling, pulling back, roaring in protest. The Voice told him to open his palm.

He emerged from the mine soon after, pale-white,

clutching something. It was getting hotter in the palm of his hand, but he waited for his eyes, adjusting to the daylight, before opening his fingers. A stone, pebble-like, sat there, with a carving of an eye so hostile he dropped it, sending it rolling between the hind legs of his donkey. The donkey kicking and the lost teeth didn't matter, he was going to be rich. He wore a bloody grin. He had work to do.

•

A train arrived in Kelso, California the next day, and on it Addison Shergold. A bright, July morning, Year of Our Lord 1945. Being a stop-off for trains heading up to Las Vegas, Addison enquired with the conductor where he might grab a bite to eat while waiting for the steam-train to be watered, and a banker-engine installed for the steep hills ahead. He ended up in the *Beanery*, a restaurant for travellers and local workers alike. He ordered stew. After, he was distracted from the reading of his newspaper by the odd behaviour in front of him.

His waitress – Mary, her name badge said – was fretting about something through the window, neglecting her waitressing duties, roused only by the third, impatient chime of the cook's service bell, meals going cold. She snapped out of it, busying herself to distribute the orders, but Addison took up her disrupted vigil. A lawman was breaking up a crew of miners, seeming to take umbrage with a young man. As Addison and

Mary took turns watching the exchange, between their respective sipping and serving of coffee, the miners were moved on, and the browbeaten young man was locked in the open air strap-iron jail cells. The lawman headed for the *Beanery*.

"Coffee," said the lawman, taking a stool near Addison at the counter. He was shaking his head, unbelieving of the dealt-with ridiculousness.

"Sure." Mary had already poured, the clairvoyance of waitress and regular in action. "I know *my man* ain't been drinkin' this mornin'. You gonna tell me what he's doin' in that cage?"

The lawman inhaled the coffee's steam, "He's in there until he stops spouting gibberish. Those miners have had enough, and so have I."

"What gibberish?" Mary asked, a triple-threat of staying professional, not getting into conflict with the law, and also trying to glean information on the captivity of *her man*.

Addison was listening with a stranger's interest; it was more appealing than his paper.

"He was asking folk to help him dig up a *temple*, or a *steeple*? Or some such nonsense. Out in the dunes. Said it's got *gold*. Started insisting. Think the sun's baked his shit-for-brains," the lawman said.

"How long did he serve?" Addison chimed in.

The lawman turned on his stool to face Addison, while Mary did her best to keep her delivery friendly, asking, "I'm sorry?"

"Sounds like shell-shock. Seeing things," said Addison. "They call them *flashbacks*. More harm than good, locking him up."

"Who the hell are you?" the lawman asked.

"Just passing through," said Addison, lifting his travel bag and heading for the door.

Mary's defensive regard muted as she noticed the dollar tip he'd left. The lawman turned back to his coffee, shaking his head at this further ridiculousness.

Outside, Addison heard the first *all-aboard* call from the conductor. He had a few minutes to spare. A few minutes to show some support.

"Where'd you serve, son?" asked Addison, approaching the jail cell.

The skinny prisoner looked up from the floor, blood-shot eyes, swollen mouth. "What's it to you, old man?"

"Saw your hassle, wanted to hear your side," said Addison.

The prisoner softened, offering his arm through the cage. "Thomas Keller, sir."

A firm shake. "Addison Shergold."

"*Gold*?" Thomas muttered, but not to Addison. It was like he was listening to something in the distance.

"I've heard all the jokes. Used to call me *Golden-Boy* in the army."

Thomas grinned, revealing bloody gaps where teeth used to be. "The first war?" he asked.

"None other. They send you boys home after VE day?" Addison asked, but Thomas's grin died, his eyeline hovering to the *Beanery* window, then the distant listening again.

"Mr Shergold, I need help. My employer is expecting me with his donkey and tools. I've left them at the dunes."

"Why'd you do that?" asked Addison.

"Found something. Came back for help to dig it up."

"*All aboard* – final call!" bawled the conductor from the platform.

"Whatever you saw, it's a *flash-back*, from the war, son."

"Think I'm crazy, like them?" Thomas slumped to the floor.

"I don't." Addison glanced to the platform.

"Then help me, *Golden-Boy*."

•

Returning home from the First World War was Christmas morning without the gifts. No hero's welcome, no celebration or recognition. Just quiet. After the screaming, cracking guns and booming shells, it was the quiet that got to Addison. Like a lot of returning vets, he felt disenfranchised; the land he gave so much to protect didn't seem to know, or care, what he'd been through. No job, no sweetheart waiting for him, no family. Just a tiny vet's apartment, with its four walls, and its deafening quiet.

He'd rather be in danger and feel alive, than safe and feel nothing. Ironically enough, he couldn't even return to war. When America joined the Second World War, they needed brave men between 21 and 45. Addison had just turned 47, and looked even older. He kept seeing Uncle Sam looming down at him from posters, finger pointed, accusatorial, *I WANT YOU!* Except he didn't want Addison. No one did.

He missed being needed for something, fighting for a just cause. The adrenaline of survival, adventure, his body craved it. The only feeling which came remotely close was gambling. The thrill of winning some, and the threat of losing it all. He'd been on a pilgrimage to Vegas, the gambler's Mecca. But this sad man in the cage needed him. A new graduate of war, down and out, disrespected. That's why Addison didn't get back on the train.

"I'll get your donkey," he said.

•

It was a four hour hike to the Kelso Dunes. The barren, rocky landscape, so recurrent around California, gave way to soft, silky sands, Addison's feet sinking into them with every step, filling his shoes. He felt transported to the epic vistas of the Middle East. To that of TE Lawrence on his adventures in Arabia, or Howard Carter on a digging expedition in Egypt, both men alumni of the Great War, like him, both of whom he admired greatly. *What if the black steeple really was there?* Addison entertained, *not the delusions of a broken man, but an archaeological find.*

His right knee flared with pain, a complaint he'd ignored for months. Opting for the *it'll sort itself out* treatment rather than seeking a doctor, who may throw around hideous words like *arthritis* or *cane*. No, he'd walk it off. The dunes loomed ahead, anyway. Monolithic curves of nature. It was then that the absurdity of the situation sank in, like the sand beneath him. Not only was this a rescue mission for a *donkey*, but such a vast canvass on which to stage the theatre of rescue. What if he couldn't find it? He hadn't even considered the task as folly. He'd just gone all-in, as he would on the poker table. *Place your bets, gentlemen.*

Reality is a door-to-door salesman, knocking on the doors of dreams. It offered Addison *the needle in a haystack? Turn around and go home!* package, as well as the *go to the doctors about your knee, before you do yourself a mischief!* special offer. He wasn't buying. He was paying attention to his racing heart, and to the adrenaline in his system. He hadn't felt this pepped-up in forever. But, upon checking his pocket watch, another unwanted traveller joined him: Father Time.

3:47. Another four and a half hours of decent light, then sheer darkness. The sands of time moved around him. No necessities to make a camp, very little food and water. The journey back would take four hours itself. He had half an hour to find the donkey and leave.

Climbing the nearest, smallest (still huge) dune was the Devil's own work. Dehydrated, hungry, exhausted. Limbs – especially knee – screaming. He stumbled his way to the top. It was like standing on the spine of a behemoth amongst a herd of them. Squinting, hand above his brow, he surveyed up and down the dunes. *Tracks.* His eyes followed. A rush of victory and relief. They led to the donkey. They also led to something else: a black steeple.

•

Food, drink and rest were the obvious antidotes to hallucination. Sitting atop his climbed dune, Addison ate his packed lunch (kindly provided by Mary at the *Beanery*, overjoyed someone was helping *her man*), but the black steeple remained. Defiant to known history and logic. The steeple was no fable, and he could see why Thomas was so desperate to uncover it. To be the first in who-knows-how-long to witness its mysteries.

Two choices: take the donkey back, or start digging.

Addison had never slid down a sand dune before, but it seemed the path of least resistance. Picking up speed, he heard a deep rumbling, booming behind him. A giant's groan. He rolled onto his stomach as he reached the bottom, shifting plates of sand following him. His adrenaline rocketed, expecting to see shell impacts in the sand, roaring planes above him, enemy guns cracking on the ridge.

Nothing there.

The donkey gazed at this new arrival: *was that you, or me?* As a logical man, he decided some trick of the sand, millions of moving grains, caused a bizarre aural phenomena he'd just played audience to. *They call them flashbacks…*

On his feet, brushing off the sand, the black steeple (still there) loomed over him, sending a frisson of chill amid hot excitement. Up close, it wasn't black, it was a veritable obsidian. It cast a shadow on him, jutting out of a much smaller dune than the one he'd scaled, but still the size of a whale. Not wood, or stone, or any material Addison could fathom; it had a dense glass-like appearance, intricately chiselled. He approached the donkey, patted its side.

"I'm here to take you home, girl."

The donkey, pleased with this, scraped a hoof in approval. One of its sides carried a saddlebag, the other, some tools: a spade, gold-pan and a packed-up tent.

The saddlebag was empty… no, something lay at the bottom. A stone. Addison retrieved it and was met with the most scowling image of an eye he'd ever seen. He thought he heard a muffled voice, distant, like it was underground. The donkey stirred. He dropped the stone back in the bag. It wasn't his to take, and he certainly didn't want it.

Decision time.

He looked at his pocket watch. If he left now he could beat the dark back to Kelso. He'd confess what he'd found, Thomas would take a team to dig up the site, press would come to take photos, hands would be shaken and history would be made. While Addison gambled away his pension in Vegas.

No. This was Addison's moment to be like Howard Carter, unearthing lost history, finding *Wonderful Things*. This was the adventure, not delivering a donkey.

Reality's salesman rapped on the door of his archaeological fantasy with a last-chance-to-buy offer. He wasn't in. He was digging.

•

Using torn up strips of the tent, and its pegs, Addison constructed a horseshoe-shaped dam around the back of the steeple. It stopped any sliding sand above replacing any he dug out below. It wasn't perfect, but it did the trick. Sand was bunching up against the tent's taut fabric. It could cause a sand-slide if it came undone, so he dug fast. Another stroke of ingenuity was using the gold-pan, rather than spade, its shape scooping larger volumes. Every so often, he crawled up behind his dam, emptying built up sand, when the tent fabric strained. Digging showed no mercy on his knee, but he'd dug out trenches under far worse duress.

He'd made significant progress, when he came to an opening in all four sides of the architecture: a belfry, sans bell. He was now digging *inside* the structure, assuming the whole thing to be packed with sand. Unless there was a trapdoor?

The sun was lost behind the dunes, the first inky-blue strokes of night surrounded him. Luckily, an oil-lamp hung amongst the tools. He lit it, hanging it on the nearest tent peg and doubled his pace, digging deeper into the cramped steeple.

The desert was jet-black outside his sphere of soft light

when he reached a flat surface. His dry hands fumbled through the grains, brushing and patting, until something rattled. A ring-pull handle for a trapdoor. He gripped it, expecting more sand underneath, and pulled.

A stale foist, carried on a gush of air pressure, was the first thing to hit Addison. The only sand in there was small streams pouring in from around him. Snatching the oil lantern, he lowered it into the haze, revealing steps, spiralling down. He swallowed, his dry throat clicking. By this time the donkey – still with him – was down on its haunches resting, *you're not really going down there, are you?*

He was, and he did, his footfalls clicking down the dull acoustics of the steeple's hollow, lantern held out like a Victorian butler answering the door to a night-time caller. Deeper, deeper. He took his time, struggling with his knee. The stale smell more acrid the further down he travelled. The steps finally widened out, revealing an opening around a final turn. He was Howard Carter, ready for *Wonderful Things.*

A sizeable nave spread before him, still obsidian-like material, no windows to let in stray sand. It was incredible such a structure could defiantly hold together under tonnes and tonnes of earth. A chill set over Addison, his sweat cooling. In the centre of this nave was a circular gathering of chairs, fixed around an alter-like centre-piece. On it, a large ceremonial plate, piled with something. Stood aghast, unable to will his legs forward, the lantern shook in his hands, bouncing shadows around the already eerie space.

He felt like an unwanted visitor, standing in the doorway. Above the altar hung a large bell, much too large for the belfry. Why was it so close to ground level? Perhaps the belfry had been a watchtower. A few unsteady steps, and he could make out what was piled on the plate. Gold.

It was the only wondrous thing in the room, the precious metal reflecting the lantern's light brighter. At the far end of the nave, Addison could now see a large double-door, an entrance, with knolls of sand at its foot, the only grains able to breach the room through cracks.

Closer inspection of the bell revealed dismaying things. Things causing Addison to place the lantern on the altar, make the gesture of the cross on his chest, and back into one of the old surrounding chairs.

The bell displayed intricate carvings, images of archaic worship to some blasphemous deity. Something serpent-like, a long curling body with a crocodile's grin. It was biting the head from one of its followers. The imagery appalled him. He suddenly felt very alone, very cold and very tired, in such an ugly, oppressive place. Like an excited child after a day's play in the hot sun, drained of energy and enthusiasm for adventure, longing for bath and bed, to be tucked in to sweet dreams. Between heavy eyelids opening and closing, Addison noticed the bell creature's eyes – *the stone in the saddlebag*, he thought. *I'll just rest a moment, that's all.*

•

In the moments after sleep, but before eyes opening, Addison assumed he was in his armchair, safe in his apartment. He was perplexed to find he wasn't; he was still sat in a cold, uncomfortable chair in that dark nave, watching Thomas Keller and Mary pack the altar's gold into saddlebags.

"Thomas?" Addison's voice echoed.

Thomas and Mary both jumped, turning from their glistening hoard. Thomas ignored Addison, doubling down his efforts, snatching the last few clumps of gold.

"He is alive."

"Shut *up*, Mary – take this up to the donkey," Thomas barked, handing her his bag.

She nodded, dashing for the spiral steps, stopping to look at Addison, before disappearing.

Addison tried to get to his feet, but his aching body – primarily his knee – insisted he stayed seated.

"Thought you'd died. After all that digging," Thomas said. "I brought her..." He nodded upwards. "...in case you'd not stuck around."

It was like being brought algebra for breakfast in bed. Addison's bleary head could make no sense of it. His lantern, still on the altar, flickered and dimmed, fighting on with a dribble of oil.

Thomas raised his pickaxe into the air. "I deserve this. For what I've been through." He home-run swung it into the bell.

The result was a monolithic chime of the deep, sending a sonic wave into Addison's being. His ears rung, eyes watered, forced shut to the cacophony. An assault of the senses, dizzying and hair-raising. By the time he opened his eyes, palms pressed tight over his ears, Thomas was gone. The bell swung in its frame, still resonating. Then a new sound. A rumbling in the deep. The sound of earth being moved. It crescendoed, making the seat beneath Addison vibrate. Then there was an impossible knock at the door behind him.

More like a crash.

Addison, still reeling from the bell, turned to see the large, double-doors straining, splitting, and another crash. Grains of sand spilled through the widening crack between the door's panels. *They call them flashbacks, right, Addison?*

His body came around to the idea of moving. He darted for the spiral steps, but passing the altar, a searing hot slash of pain stopped him. After fifty one years of function, Addison's right anterior cruciate ligament decided to part ways with his knee-cap. His chest broke the fall, chin grazing, teeth clacking together, just as his lantern gave up the ghost, flickering, snuffing him into pure darkness. A final mighty crash brought the doors down, behind him. Sand poured and hissed, piling in. Then something else hissed, and slithered.

An ancient, survivalist instinct pushed aside Addison's sanity. It took over the controls. No cohesive thought, just scrambling limbs, ripped fingernails and lacerated flesh in the primordial need to reach those steps and live on. The chime of the bell, and crash of the empty plate echoed, as whatever came through the door reached the altar. The guttural shrieks and bellows echoing after Addison as he hopped and thrashed up the steps were only surpassed in repugnance by the smell of its breath following him, the smell of absolute death.

Once the hopping, thrashing fight to reach the spiral's top was won, a new problem introduced itself, as Addison's head cracked into it. The trap door was shut-tight. He pounded his fists and shoulders, roaring, but it wouldn't yield. His sand dam must have given-way, burying the small belfry, entombing him.

The steeple began to shake with cracking, splitting sounds as the creature beneath (*the bell creature*), clearly unable to fit into the steeple's spiral, struggled and fought, rumbling the architecture. Addison was thrown side to side, tumbling back down the steps. The wall became the floor, as gravity pulled him sideways amidst a mighty *cracking*. Bones broke, all sense of direction lost, tumbling inside this rolling tube, like the last candy in the jar, shaken by a greedy child.

Then, breeze on his face, the smell of sand. He crawled, following these sensations, until he felt sand on his bloody palms. He was out, at the foot of the dunes. He crawled to the edge of the steeple's demolition and saw a hazy light in the distance, to the flank of the much larger dunes ahead. The image wavered and danced, but squinting, he made it out to be the donkey, Thomas and Mary guiding it, by lamplight. There was a commotion;

the donkey bucked and struggled, spooked by something. It reared. He could hear it heehawing.

With minimal light from the distant lantern, and eyes now acclimatised, Addison saw the shape of the dunes pulsing, the creature swimming through them, the sands groaning and booming. Thomas and Mary were trying to calm the donkey's bucking and heehawing. The movement in the dunes was heading toward them.

An eruption of sand rained on them, followed by a grinning, reptilian head bursting out like hell's jack-in-the-box, its head lolling with sickening dexterity from its sewer-pipe neck. Black-green scales, and *those eyes* – it made Addison want to throw up.

Then the screaming started.

The donkey had run for its life into the darkness ahead, leaving Thomas and Mary at the pleasures of this Triassic death-titan. They weren't eaten whole; it was messy. Several passes of snapping jaws, the lantern caught somewhere inside its gullet, illuminating how little was left of them every time it opened up for more. Addison pushed his face in the sand, holding back the worst screaming a man could make. The creature retreated, rumbling back to its deep sanctum.

•

Addison's broken, bloody, dehydrated, exhausted body lay in the darkness. His deep survivalist instinct's pilot light waning. He didn't want to die here, alone, afraid. He was *Golden-Boy*, and he'd crawled through no-man's-land in the Great War, the deck had been stacked against him so many times.

He gritted his teeth and crawled.

He clawed at the sand, dragging his dead-weight over volatile terrain. Sand was scrubbing and filling his open wounds. His dry skin cracked and split with every stretch. Broken bones grinding. If he stopped, he wouldn't be able to start again.

It was in the first moments of dawn's soft light, washing over the horizon, he heard the donkey. Heehawing somewhere ahead. He put his bloody, shaking fingers to his mouth and whistled, but his lips were too dry, sounding like a burst beach ball deflating. So he called, momentarily blacking out from the pain and effort. He awoke to the donkey's muzzle, snuffling the back of his head. Its saddlebag bulging with gold.

There was no way to get on the donkey; he couldn't stand. Improvising, he took his belt off, and with the very last of his strength, threaded the buckle, pulling it tight around his wrist, strapping the other end to the donkey's saddle. He gave the donkey a pat on the backside and was dragged away on his back.

•

The miners Thomas Keller had so offended were the ones to see the wandering donkey dragging something behind it. Hiking to an early dig, they figured they better investigate this oddity first. Initially shocked, and immediately aiding Addison, there was a gallows humour to the situation. Something they found cracked them up.

•

Bandaged tight, washed and rested, Addison woke up in the safety of the Kelso Train Depot's lodgings. A doctor had been called, and he'd been tended to in shifts by various staff from the platform and the *Beanery* over the last few days.

The lawman was leaned against the wall, his signature head shaking in full flow. "So this is 'just passing through'? You got a story to tell?"

"I don't remember anything," Addison replied, only half lying.

Those eyes.

No, he was choosing not to remember a damned thing. He planned to get out of here as soon as possible. The next train ideally, but not to Vegas. Home. To his tiny vet's apartment with his comfortable chair, and its wonderful quiet.

"Well, I'm sorry to say, whatever happened, it was all in vain, unless you're planning on starting a paper-weight business."

"I don't follow," said Addison.

"That bag-full of shiny – it was fool's gold."

•

It was after saving Addison's life and having a good laugh at the '*gold*', one of the miners heard the Voice. It told him to look deeper in the saddlebag, quiet whispers at first. He'd found a stone, a kind of pebble. Hot in his hand, it displayed the ugliest symbol of an eye.

The Voice told him there were riches, *real gold*, out there, and it was rightly his, but he must follow some instructions.

He didn't go out mining that day with the others, or the day after that. He had work to do.

•

About Nate Connor

Nate Connor is a Sunderland-based writer of Weird Fiction. You can find his first, highly commended story, Failure's Door, in the Crossing the Tees Book Festival's Second Short Story Anthology, published by Sixth Element Publishing in 2018.

Find out more at www.6e.net/nateconnor

BEYOND COMMUNICATION

MARIOS ERACLEOUS

The ferocious wind was howling like an angry wolf. Thunder crashed through the skies tearing open the heavens as lightning surged left to right across the black, rain heavy clouds. It was nothing like anything he had ever seen. Dr Harry Stevens drove through the sleepy little suburb eager to get to his warm cosy home, afraid that he would be left stranded in the middle of nowhere if the storm worsened, convinced this was the storm he'd been waiting for.

He reached his destination with a sigh of relief and scurried out of his battered old Jeep. The thunder continued to roar but louder than before, the rain coming down like bullets, and Harry slung his overcoat over his head and rushed inside.

"Dr Stevens!" Mrs Gatsby his housekeeper waddled over like a penguin helping him as she took off his coat and hung it on the peg next to the door. "There's some hot tea waiting for you in the study. Oh, your new apprentice is here." Mrs Gatsby smiled and headed back into the kitchen. She handed Harry a towel for his wet hair and he dried himself like a shaggy dog.

He stepped inside to the study where the young woman was reading one of his books entitled 'Beyond Communication' as she drank a cup of Earl Grey tea, the aroma drifting delicately into the air.

Harry coughed to grab her attention. "Your name, my dear?"

"Lynn," she smiled. "Lynn Tanner."

Her elegant looks surprised him as she shook his hand.

Harry poured himself a cup. "I understand you graduated top of your class?"

"Yes," she replied.

"A straight 'A' student, I believe?"

She nodded.

"And your hobbies include a love of science fiction?"

She blushed slightly. "Yes, well…"

"Perfect," Harry said. "You see, in our line of work, you need a certain… open mindedness, yes, open-mindedness."

The young lady smiled.

"Perfect," Harry said again, nodding away.

Lynn's cheeks glowed with excitement and her face broke into a wide beaming smile.

He hurried over to his desk with a mask of determination to find what he was looking for. Amongst the chaos of piles and piles of papers and files, he found a small key. "Mrs Gatsby!"

Mrs Gatsby peered through the door. "Yes, Doctor?"

"Can you take Lynn and show her the rest of the house for a moment please." He glanced over at her.

Then Mrs Gatsby nodded enthusiastically. "The conservatory is lovely when it's raining. Come and see."

She grabbed her niece's hand and took her away, closing the door behind them.

Harry scurried over to the other side of the room and opened a safe concealed behind a portrait. He tapped a couple of numbers into the keypad and the door swung open. He retrieved a small memory stick, kissed it, shut the door, and closed the portrait. This is it, he told himself.

Harry found Mrs Gatsby and Lynn in the kitchen, nattering away. "Are you ready?"

Lynn looked excited like a child at a sweet shop. He guided her to his workshop at the end of the garden, the rain pelting down around them.

As they entered the workshop, the lights switched on automatically. There were computer screens scattered all around the room. Lynn looked around in awe.

"This, Lynn, is where it begins. Communication with the stars." He tapped a few keys, put in the memory stick and waited. The connection was made, the signal boost transferred to the outer skies. "Pray for life beyond the stars."

"What do we do?"

He gestured towards a chair in the centre of the room, surrounded by machines, wires and monitors.

"You sit here," he said. "Quickly. I can feel that they're close."

•

Two weeks later and another tremendous storm found Max Watts sitting in his little newly-rented flat not far from the village. Max was in his early twenties, tall and slender and a bit of a geek. He sat on his sofa, the acceptance letter for his new job on the coffee table in front of him – a position at a new high tech firm, not one he'd heard of before. He knew he was taking a risk, but it'd sounded too exciting to pass. He was due to start on Monday. The time now? Nine thirty on a Friday evening. Max was feeling tired and falling asleep. But he'd just unpacked his vast collection of movies, his favourites ranging from those featuring monsters and outer space to wonderfully weird conspiracy theories.

Engrossed in the latest blockbuster, flashing images and graphics galore on his massive 65" state of the art smart TV screen, a vast roaring sound came from above the clouds as if something had ripped open the very heavens.

"What the…?" yelled Max and he hurried to his window. Looking towards the sky, he spied a huge beam of bright lights heading to the other side of the village.

•

Harry heard an alarm going off. "We got something," he called. He grabbed his laptop and switched it on immediately. "Come on, come on," he said impatiently. "There – the other side of the village." He grabbed his bag, keys and headed for the door. "Mrs Gatsby, put the kettle on!"

•

Max paused for a moment until the rapid beat of his heart calmed. There were no lights to guide him to his whereabouts and he was out of breath. The local woodland area was silent, an eerie silence prevailing as if something was waiting in the dark, holding its breath. Max ventured deeper into the forest.

Lights beamed from the bushes. There was a sudden movement, and the sound of rustling filled the air. Slowly the light shone towards him, getting brighter and brighter. Max was stunned. He gasped. And keeled over.

•

Max opened his eyes to find himself sitting on a couch, feeling slightly dumfounded. Two people were looking at him.

"Oh good, you're awake," the man said. "Mrs Gatsby, make yourself useful. Go and get him a tea, will you?"

The older lady, apparently Mrs Gatsby, headed out of the door.

"Now," said the scruffy looking man in front of Max as he pulled up a chair and sat opposite. "My name is Dr Harry Stevens." He picked up a file from his nearby desk and flipped it open. "Max Watts, IT analyst and sci-fi nut, I see from your CV." He closed the file and smiled. "Seems that you'll be starting your new job with us a little earlier than Monday. So what did you see in the woods?"

Mrs Gatsby came back and handed Max a cup of tea that smelled strange, one of those weird teas like Earl Grey. He tried a smile and groaned a little. The old lady reassured him and made him drink a little tea. He slowly told the doctor everything, hesitating in places. Mrs Gatsby was by his side and that made him feel relaxed. Like having a mother figure next to him at a surgery or getting an injection from the nurse. He told Harry how the lights shone brighter than the sun itself and its sound was like a vast flying saucer. "The lights… how could I forget those lights. It was like a great big shining star."

Max looked around him and the darkened room turned brighter as a laboratory came into view complete with gadgets, gizmos aplenty and a huge computer screen.

"Where am I?" Max asked as he took in the sight. He placed the tea to one side, stood and walked around and imagined all he could achieve by being there. He ran his hand over furniture, keyboards and screens.

"Now you've seen everything, Max. It's important that we find these aliens again." Harry swung his chair to face the monitor. "Computer on."

The computer switched itself on as lights beamed around it.

"Authorisation needed." A woman's face materialised on the screen.

"Doctor Harry Stevens," he called.

"What…?" Max exclaimed, his eyes wide with excitement.

Harry turned to Max who was looking amazed.

"It's okay." Harry turned to his new acquaintance. "Computer, can you show the images of tonight's apparitions please?"

The computer image disintegrated and images flooded the screen.

"This is what you saw in the woods?"

The young man nodded, all of it coming back to him. "The lights, the lights were gleaming so bright." The sweat began to pour from his forehead as if he had just done a two hundred metre run.

"Okay, take it easy, my boy, take it easy," urged Harry. "Computer, off."

The computer closed itself down.

"So what do you think the lights are then?" asked Max.

"They are not from here and they are definitely not military," Harry suggested. "They will be coming back and we need to be ready for them. The storm is building. You'd best stay the night."

•

Harry carried on working, keeping himself up with caffeine. He tapped away at the computers, listening through the communication device, hoping to find the next signal, watching the storm reports, looking for a sign.

"You're not asleep." Mrs Gatsby's voice startled him as he turned to her.

"I can't. We're so close… I can feel it. I can feel the elements coming together, First Lynn, now Max… Listen to this. They are like radio waves. Can you hear it, Mrs Gatsby?"

"Do we need to try again?"

Harry nodded. "Get it ready."

•

Max tossed and turned. He woke up sweating and reached for a glass of water, downing it quickly. He got up and got dressed, slowly stepping out onto the landing, downstairs and out of the cottage for a little fresh air. He noticed the workshop lights were on. He looked at his watch: 3am.

He hurried over to the workshop and turned the door handle, and let himself in. He saw Doctor Stevens, working away at the computers.

"I couldn't sleep," he said softly. "I had a nightmare. I felt I was with them."

Harry turned to him. "With them?"

"Up there," he said. "You think I'm dumb."

Harry shook his head. "No, no, I think we are onto something." He clasped his hands together then took

Max by the arm to guide him to the centre of the room where there was a chair surrounded by machinery and wires, lights flashing.

"Max, lie here and don't worry," Harry said.

Max settled uneasily into the seat.

"This," Harry said, "is the key to communicating with them. You have the power to bring them to us through your extraordinary mind." Harry touched Max's cheek, offering some comfort. He then strapped Max's arms to the armrests and secured gadgets on either side of his head.

"The wave patterns will begin an electromagnetic pulse, which will travel through your body. Just stay calm. Here we go." Harry smiled. He switched on the button and flows of energy travelled through the mind of the young man. "Come on, come on," he urged as a sudden jerk of movement came from him.

"Harry," Mrs Gatsby shouted.

He turned as the waves showed up on screen.

"Mrs Gatsby, they are here, they are here." He rushed outside into the open air and a gleam of light appeared above him. The light shone, glistening all around and he stared in awe and wonder.

The light shimmered and faded.

•

Two weeks later, Alex Reynolds peered through her window, staring out at the vicious storm, hoping it wasn't set in for the weekend. She'd just moved to this little village, new job and all, starting Monday, exciting new tech firm by the sound of it, and the Internet connection in her new apartment had been surprisingly impressive until the storm hit.

There was a crash of lightning and the power cut, all seven high res monitor screens showing scenes from the real time online multi-player sci-fi action game she was playing all blinking off in an instant, leaving her in total darkness. Lights appeared in the sky above the woods on the edge of the village.

Strange, she thought, strangely compelled to follow them.

She walked out into the torrential rain… the forest floor was soft under her bare feet. She didn't jump as a hand touched her arm.

"Come with me," a voice said.

•

She opened her eyes, head foggy as if she'd been drugged. She was in some kind of workshop or laboratory. Outside the thunder rumbled ever louder, crashes of unearthly energy colliding boomed right overhead. Alex looked around. There, in the centre of the lab, surrounded by machinery, lights blinking in a frenzy, was a chair…

A motherly voice to her left made her turn. "Earl Grey?"

About Marios Eracleous

Nursery Nurse by day and a writer by night, Marios has written many stories and web serials over the year. His passion for sci-fi comes from his love of the worlds brought to life in British and US cult classic TV, especially Doctor Who and Star Trek. He enjoys reading sci-fi, thrillers and historical fiction.

Find out more at www.6e.net/marioseracleous

THE PROMISE

PAUL GOODCHILD

There is something I need to hold on to, something I have to remember.

I am alone. Trapped in an endless void, without even a mouth to voice my outrage. I don't know how long I've been here, days perhaps, or decades. I peer into the void, searching for answers in the dark, and the void stares back with grey, ancient eyes. They can not help me, they are as lost and afraid as I am, but at least I am not alone.

In the distance, a light flares, spewing out a torrent of ochre static that drives away the darkness. I feel my body, weighed down with the dull ache of age. The sensation is fleeting, slipping away as the light envelops me, replaced with a vision that melts into being around me.

I find myself in a busy nightclub, all flashing lights and glaring displays. I see a young man. He is dancing, his body flowing with the beat as he sashays across the dance floor, the glowing tiles pulsing to the beat of some long forgotten tune. His attention is fixed on a figure in a fitted tux, their shirt glowing under the black light as they mirror his farcical procession into the centre of the club. The dancer glides toward them, slipping easily past the other revellers, a graceful procession that comes crashing down in a tangled heap, wiped out by a drunk who was too keen to get their tray of lurid shots to their friends.

A chaos of static overexposes the scene, and the vision fails, losing focus in the distortion. His mind, or my mind, wanders. Adrift in the void, it is difficult to tell one from the other. Again, I sense the ghost of my body, skulking in and out of my perception. I feel the whine of an electric saw, and the dull edge of anaesthetised agony.

The figure in the fitted tux is a light in the void, guiding me back to the vision. I see Dancer, still in the club, empty now except for him and Tux. Tux has changed, their clothes struggling to contain a frame fattened by happiness, their alluring confidence suppressed by nerves. They lower themself carefully to one knee and produce a glittering steel band that dances in the light. They hold it up to Dancer in trembling hands and the club fades, the entire vision focusing down on Tux, their grey eyes wide, beautiful, and full of hope. Dancer laughs, fumbling a scarlet box from his pocket and kneeling with them, never taking his eyes from theirs. "Marry me," they say in unison. In my bodiless state, their love pulls at me, and I am unmoved.

I hear a voice, the words lost to me, and my focus shifts in an instant. I am lying in a bare hospital bed, the spindly arms of some great machine retreating out of my view and folding themselves into a stained housing on the ceiling. A steel man lies on the bed next to mine, his unmoving body is worn, ancient and empty. Confused, I scan my surroundings. The room is part surgical suite, part engineer's workshop. One wall is taken up by an abstract painting, a mess of shapes that refuses to resolve into a recognisable whole. I am sure it is looking at me. I clamber uncertainly out of the hospital bed and stretch, my shell stiff, the joints clogged with their first coating of lubricant. It will be months before they'll wear to a comfortable fit, years before they need replacing. I feel new, like a child again.

The thought summons another vision, and I see Dancer again, playing with a little boy. He is chasing him round on his hands and knees, the little one's exuberant waddle stalling as he checks his father is still there. Dancer scoops his son up, planting a kiss on his head that elicits a rolling giggle, and the simple joy of it melts my heart. It is truly something to hold on to.

Back in my new shell, I realise I can't remember my name. I probe at its absence, a sucking void where certainty should reside. I try to distract myself from it, picturing the face of my love, but find only a vague blur around grey eyes that refuses to resolve. I pound my fists into the bed in frustration, leaving dents the size of apples in the steel frame.

"Wa," a voice calls out, startling me. "Waaa," it repeats, the sound drawn out, lethargic.

There is something I need to remember. The vision blots out the world again, and I see Dancer, drowning in impotent sadness, wrenched away from the sweetest of memories and plunged into the most bitter. Tux stands next to him, and I wonder how one person can hold so much grief. An old man is lying in a hospital bed before them, sustained by tubes and gently beeping machines. They kneel on either side of the bed and hold the old man's hands. His tissue-thin skin is peppered with liver spots, so different from the synthetic skin on the lovers' hands, the type of silly affectation I've grown beyond. They stay there, whispering to the old man for a time, before Tux lets out a heaving sob, their slight frame buckling under the weight of it, and rushes from the room in a cloud of broken composure. As Tux leaves, the vision fades, leaving only the echo of the dying man's weak voice. "Don't leave me, Dad," he begs.

I am back by the dented hospital bed, and the mechanical voice is still trying to piece itself together. "Wata, waa, wata," it repeats. I ignore it, and stumble to the steel man on legs rendered clumsy by unfamiliarity. He is battered, possessing a beauty formed of skilful, careful repair, and long, heavy use. His faithful body is lifeless, like a discarded toy, the empty eyes unfocused and unblinking. I kneel by his side, and trace the patina of age with a silver digit, the memories of my recent life knitting together, reordering into a sense of self. How I long to see my love again. I try to call her face to mind, and fall back into memory.

Dancer is sitting with Tux, the pair garbed in black, right down to their prosthetics. They are alone in a garden of remembrance, two grieving parents lost in endless sorrow. Together they consider everything they have lost, weighing the cost of their collective decision. Would they go back, even if they could?

"Promise me," says Tux, fixing Dancer with their grey eyes. "Promise me you will never die," they insist, still beautiful, even in their deepest grief. "Promise you won't leave me too."

"I promise, I will never leave you," I say, the words appearing on my lips unbidden, mirroring Dancer's, the memory integrating into my own, another piece slotting into place.

My personality is taking shape now, and gazing at the faceplate of the steel man I find myself recognising my old shell. A steel corpse with my face. I reach down and lift off the faceplate. It comes away easily, loosened in preparation for my transfer. I turn it over in new hands, marvelling at the intricate engraving I made, how it catches the light and seems to move of its own accord. The beauty of a craft honed over centuries, and now lost to me. So personal, and yet so alien. I wonder when I lost my humanity.

The vision comes to me easily, a memory of ingenious machinery freeing the seat of my consciousness from its fleshy prison and crowning it in immortal steel. It is a moment of triumph, marred by intense grief. A grief whose source eludes me still. There is something I have to remember.

Resigned to my duty, I stand, taking a single pace back from my old shell. I bow deeply, grateful for its service. Prostrate, I slide the faceplate into place with shaking hands, and it locks perfectly into place. Completing my ritual. I pull myself up straight, head held high by an invisible string, the rigid posture of the faithful warrior. A steel man steadfastly carrying out his forgotten duty.

I notice the voice has sped up, looping on itself as it struggles to speak in a language I no longer recognise. I listen for a while as it repeats itself, over and over, the same few syllables, getting stronger each time. "Watash, watashi, watashi wa, watash, watashi wa," it babbles.

I lose track of the voice and find myself carrying someone down a corridor dripping with photographs and keepsakes. The faces in the photographs as unfamiliar to me as the withered, incomplete being in my hands. Its grey eyes stare past me, unfocused and empty. We turn into a bedroom filled with the pulsing, wheezing machinery of life, and I lay them down on a single bed that is separated from its neighbour by just a few inches of empty space. They stir as I withdraw, a flash of presence sparking as I tuck them in with firm and meticulous care, their beautiful grey eyes fixing on my own, anchoring me in place.

"Bury me in my tux, husband. Lay me down by our son," Tux pleads.

"Of course, my love," I reply, reassuring them of their place at rest.

"And remember your promise," Tux demands with a force of clarity that drills into me, their one absolute in the fog.

"I promise, I will never die," I repeat. The same promise I make every night. I wish I had known then that this is the last time I get to make it in person. That the disease will finally snatch my love away from me, leaving me to walk this endless path alone, and dance no more.

I find myself standing before the portrait again, seeing it anew, a giant abstract three feet tall. It observes my every motion, the indistinct face framing piercing grey eyes that follow me around the room.

"Watashi wa Ika, wata, watashi, watashi wa Ikara," the voice tries again, and I know there is something I have to hold on to. I find myself sitting alone, surrounded by the ghosts of my life. Pictures of people I no longer recognise stare at me from virgin walls, moved into my new abode more out of habit than sentiment. I have no time for people who sit idly in misery, or those that flounder without purpose. It is time I held myself to the same standard.

Gathering every scrap of clutter, I arrange the ghosts into piles. Anyone I cannot match, or do not recognise, I stack in the empty fireplace, a teetering mound of lost memory. All but two faces find their way onto the pile. The first is a man, his short stack of photographs are faded, battered in spite of the great care lavished upon them. I arrange them in sequence, a baby growing into a boy, maturing into a man, and succumbing to time in seven photographs, highlights carefully curated by tearful grey eyes. It is the same boy I remember playing with, the same man that lay dying before me in my bitterest memory. My son. I want to crawl back into the void, but the memory is merciless, and it presses on, forcing me to the next face. There is only a hologram here, a looping recording, my grey-eyed love and I laughing our way through a series of ever sillier dances, promenading across grey tiles in the first swell of love.

Fire glows into life at the end of a match and scours away my lost memories. The burning mementos cast my new shrine in a flickering orange light that brings the photographs to life, a boy, no longer forgotten, dancing with his parents once more. A reminder of what we lost, and the cost of my promise.

"Watashi wa Ikarashi Toshiro, wata, watashi wa," the voice drones at me, and I grasp at a new memory, drawing it into myself. I am alone, standing in an overgrown cemetery. The gravestones before me are ancient, the engravings long since worn away from the moss flecked marble. I don't need them, the words are etched on my soul.

"Here lies," I recite to myself. But here lies who?

"Here lies," I try again, probing for the name of my love, and the name of our son. They are gone. Lost to time, another casualty of my endless duty. I feel a great pain at their loss, but it makes no difference, the promise endures.

"Watashi wa Ikarashi Toshiro," the voice repeats itself one last time, and I finally recognise it as my own, speaking in a forgotten tongue, long unused.

"Watashi wa shinanai," the voice finishes.

Anchored in the present, I turn to the image of my love. "My name is Ikarashi Toshiro, I will never die," I vow, my new shell bowing to the portrait, a promise remade to a love long since lost.

•

About Paul Goodchild

Paul Goodchild is a stay at home dad who amuses himself by writing stories about the limits of humanity. You can find him on twitter @uploadedwriter.

Find out more at www.6e.net/paulgoodchild

ALAN SHAW AND THE FINAL FLIGHT

CRAIG HALLAM

June 1862
Chicago, USA

Warmed by a generous early morning sun, the breeze blew in from Lake Michigan's nearby shoreline to tussle Alan's blond mop of hair and tug at his tan duster. Acres of fresh grassland spread around him with Chicago's skyline just a hazy impression in the distance. It should have been idyllic, blissful, if it weren't for the fact that he was staring down at the lid of a cheap coffin as it receded into the ground.

By his side, Merry shifted her weight from foot to foot and brushed a wave of dark blonde hair behind an ear. Neither of them was really dressed for the occasion, Alan in his armoured waistcoat and tatty coat, Merry in her air-corps issue jumpsuit, flight goggles perched atop her head. But their attendance had been a hurried thing. Privateers rarely had time for ceremony.

Neither of them wept, but they were solemn. The grave's new inhabitant was a worrying example of what might be for people in their line of work. The church service had been brief, but at the graveside the priest continued to drone on, accompanied by the sound of ropes on wood, shifting earth and Alan's impatient sighs.

"And so, we commit to the ground the body of our brother, Harrison Stanhope. May his spirit live on beside God, our father, and his son, Lord Jesus Christ…"

"Some of the living still have a bloody job to do," Alan muttered in gritted-teeth cockney.

Merry's elbow connected with his rib.

"…Let us say a final prayer."

Alan rolled his eyes as Merry bowed her head.

The bar was nothing but a hole in the ground with a counter, behind which a barman with a vibrant orange chin beard sauntered back and forth, a rag slung over his shoulder. It reminded Alan of pubs back home in London where bringing your customers straight to the beer cellar was the height of efficiency.

As with the graveside, Alan and Merry were the only ones there. This early in the morning, chairs were still tucked neatly under tables, the bar only a little sticky. Sliding his scotch glass across the wooden surface, Alan clinked it with Merry's untouched glass, and knocked it back. After a second or two, Merry drank hers as well.

"You're quiet," Alan said.

"You're supposed to be quiet at a wake," Merry said,

her accent a lilting northern English. She waved to the barman for another drink.

They sat in silence for a little longer before, with a sigh, Merry shook herself.

"Right, that's enough. We've got a job to do so let's do it," she said, pulling a tri-folded letter from her jumpsuit. Spreading her Letter of Marque on the bar, she read it again. "What do we know?" She sighed deeply as she searched for something, anything, extra in the sparsely written letter.

To those parties externally addressed,

With the receipt of this document, you are hereby requested to attend upon work of the highest importance by this honourable office. The work in question requires investigation into the death of a fellow freelance employee of this office, Harrison Stanhope. Mr Stanhope was found dead in his Chicago abode on the 10th of June. The funeral service for Mr Stanhope will take place at Rosehill Cemetery, Chicago, USA, on the 16th of June.

Yours faithfully,

The letter signed off with a flourish that might have read '*Rook*'.

Although the letter was formal, Alan couldn't help smirking at how little information was actually present. No sender, no return address, certainly no mention of the word Privateer or a method of payment, only the implied and subtle and guarded. Then the name, of course, which Alan was one-hundred percent sure wasn't what it said on Rook's birth certificate. It was certainly no accident that Her Majesty's spy-clerk had sent Harrison's case to Alan and Merry. Despite the distant wording of the letter, Rook knew this would be personal for them.

"Not much, as usual. He mentions Harrison's apartment," Alan said, tapping a finger on the sentence. "That's about as heavy handed as I've ever seen Rook be. He must be going soft in his old age."

Merry nodded. "That's a good start."

Stools scraping on the bar's flagstone floor, they made to leave. Alan dropped some bank notes on the bar with no real idea of how much they'd spent, but the barkeep didn't chase them. Up narrow stairs to the bustling Chicago streets, Alan couldn't help but feel entirely out of his depth. The roads were clogged with a mix of hurtling steam-cabs and daredevil cyclists. Everyone and everything seemed to be in a rush, and Alan had no idea who anyone was. Back home in London, you could tell the toffs from the paupers, the thugs from the coppers. Here, it wasn't so easy. There was only the throng and wide streets running in frustratingly straight lines. That was how Americans thought, Alan mused, and certainly how Harrison worked. Always in straight lines. He had to wonder if that was what got him killed, or just bad luck. It didn't take much of a misstep to turn fatal in the world of a Privateer. Alan had scars to prove it, and not all of them were external.

He trailed after Merry, whose sense of direction was impeccable. As a pilot, her perspective was always from above, every city they visited just another map in her head. In short order, she led them to the foot of a multi-storey cuboid decorated with small windows.

"How do you know this is it?" he asked. "All buildings look the damned same, here."

But she was already heading inside.

The elevator's concertina door rammed home as Merry clicked the huge lever to the gold-embossed number three and, with a shudder, they began to rise. Merry led them down a corridor which Alan thought might be vaguely familiar. It had been a year or so and beyond the veil of alcohol when he'd last been here. It had been a job well done, and a deserved celebration, that much he remembered. Harrison had drunkenly refused to let them get a hotel.

Even Alan could have spotted the right door. The police notice pasted to the bare wood suggested they were about to do something illegal. They didn't even break stride as they walked into the apartment and closed the door behind them.

"Door's in one piece," Alan said.

"I noticed that. They definitely didn't bust in."

A little light cut into the small room through a slatted blind above a writing bureau. It had been left open, papers spewing from it and onto the floor. The sagging old chair beneath the lamp where Alan had once drunkenly passed out was now on its side. The narrow cot where Merry had slept had also been overturned and the contents of the shoeboxes beneath coated the threadbare carpet.

Merry moved into the room, silently, and began hunting around. Alan ducked through the tiny apartment's only doorway to a kitchen the size of a changing cubicle, and clambered over the pots and broken crockery to get to a poor excuse for a bathroom beyond. The bath had been where Harrison had slept that night so long ago. He'd needed to be close to the well-stained toilet for his own purposes. Alan gave a smile at the memory of ribbing the American over losing his stomach, which merged into a tightened jaw and prickling eyes. He turned away and, clearing his throat, called out to Merry.

"Unless they fought each other in every room in the place, I think our villain was looking for something," Alan shouted through. "Can't imagine what it might have been. For a Privateer, Harrison lived like a tramp. Found anything?"

"Actually, yes."

Perched on the upended chair, Merry stared at another Letter of Marque. She began to read it aloud. "*To those parties externally addressed. With the receipt of this document, you are hereby requested to attend upon work of the highest importance by this honourable office. The work in question requires the acquisition…*"

"Stealing," Alan interrupted.

"*…of a series of blueprints from the esteemed engineer, Baxter Moore, who resides in Chicago, USA. Also, the prototype of the aforementioned work. I'm certain that you will be able to identify the items in question upon arrival. The items should be acquired prior to June 10th. Yours faithfully…*"

"Let me guess," Alan said. "Rook."

Tight lipped, Merry nodded. "That bastard. Send him on a job that gets him killed, send us after the killer. It's obviously this engineer. Shouldn't be too hard to find him."

Alan headed for the door, but Merry didn't follow.

"Alan, do you ever think about dying?"

He stopped dead, looked back over his shoulder.

"Don't talk daft."

"Even in the air corps, I never really thought about it. But, we've seen a lot of Privateers die over the last couple of years. We don't have much of a life expectancy. It makes you think, doesn't it?"

"Not much can make me think," he quipped. But the smile he gave her was soaked up by eyes that were all too hollow. Crossing the room, he took a knee next to her. "What's gotten into you, kid? This is just a job, you know. That letter? We can ignore it if you want. We'll take the glider, just go somewhere. Let Rook sort out his own mess."

"I don't want to do that. It isn't about Rook. You know?"

He nodded. "I know."

"I need to shake myself."

"What do you say we go punch an engineer? You'll feel better."

She gave a smile, but it was a weak one. "Let's find this bastard," she said.

"That's more like it!"

Thud.

They both startled, whipping their heads toward the window. A heavy creak from beyond the blinds and the sound of rushing of air. Light poured in through the slats where there been little before; something had been blocking it.

Drawing his revolver from its shoulder holster, Alan darted for the window. Meeting Merry there, they threw up the window together and leaned out. But there was nothing to see. Only the squirming masses in the street below, and the sunlight over a smoke-choked Chicago skyline.

"Pigeons," Alan snorted.

As he went to move away, Merry grabbed his shoulder.

"Big bloody pigeons," she said, gesturing to the windowsill where two splintered chunks were missing from the wood.

The night in Chicago was no better than the day. Between fizzing streetlamps and the blinding headlights of steam-cabs, the street was a pulsing, melodramatic light show. Alan ducked back into the alley, squeezing his eyes shut as another bright beam hit him square in the face. Back in the shadows, Merry was eyeing the warehouse across the street, her eyes narrow, chewing her lip as she pondered.

"If he's in there, he'll see us coming easily," she said. "We stick out like a sore thumb."

"Whatever happened to the early hours when everyone goes to damned sleep and it's quiet?" Alan muttered as he checked the triple dials of his wristwatch. It was well past midnight. A small chattering group sauntered past the alley entrance, oblivious to the Privateers watching them. "All electric light has done is made people nocturnal. It used to be that the only ones out at night were nutters and coppers. You might get stabbed, but you could sneak around, at least. Bloody technology has made our jobs a lot harder."

"Maybe we don't need to sneak," Merry said, stepping up beside him. She looked down the street, where the group of strangers was moving away. "We need to change our approach a bit. Put your arm around me."

Alan cocked his head, confused.

Grabbing his arm, she draped it over her shoulder.

"Put your arm around me. We're going for a walk."

They set off, Merry snuggled under Alan's armpit, her hand wrapped around his waist. Alan nuzzled in, resting his chin on her head so that they were contorted, struggling to walk sensibly, the very visage of awkward infatuation.

"You're a bit too good at this," Merry said.

"Shut up, darling, sweetest. Laugh a bit and we'll sell it more."

Merry laughed, but gave him a dig in the ribs as well.

Their ruse was good enough. They crossed the street, halting as cabs hurtled by within inches of them, their awkward affection ignored by anyone who spotted them, and turned down the opposite sidewalk so that they could pass by the warehouse's front doors. Alan leant in, kissing the top of Merry's head, which drew his eyes in line to stare right in through the warehouse's lower window as they passed.

"I can't see much," he said. "But there's no lights on."

"Good. C'mere, Loverboy."

Grabbing his duster, Merry dragged him into the alley beside the warehouse just as another couple passed by, giving knowing smirks. Alan's back hit the warehouse wall. Merry pressed against him.

"Hellfire, Merry, steady on."

"I want you, I need you," she said without a lick of emotion.

"I want my spine in one piece as well, if you don't mind."

Merry pressed her head to his chest as if listening to the loving patter of his heart, while looking out into the street.

"No one even looked. See? That was easy. Your heart's beating a bit fast, Al."

Taking Merry by the shoulders, Alan backed her up a step and went about straightening his clothes.

"Just the excitement of the job."

She gave him a teasing smile, flicking her finger under his chin. "Obviously."

Taking one last look out at the street, Alan followed Merry into the dark.

The warehouse was only one part of a sprawling complex of lesser buildings that huddled on the western side of the city. Swiftly made, without any character or soul, they were simply large brick boxes for storing smaller wooden ones. At the rear, between a refuse pile and the empty metal can that it should have inhabited, they found a rear door. Merry stepped aside to let Alan through. Pressing one ear to the door, he tried the doorknob but it wouldn't budge.

"It's a sad state, the world's in," he said, reaching into his duster pocket for a pair of fine metal tools. "No one trusts anyone anymore."

It took a little work, but he finally convinced the lock as Merry watched the darkness. The inside of the warehouse smelled of glue and sawdust with the odd undertone of oil. His lockpicks stowed safely, Alan slid one hand under his armpit and produced his revolver. Merry followed behind, looking back as much as she did forward as they crept between high shelving units bearing unmarked crates and tubes. Reaching the end of the row, Alan paused. He looked back for Merry, who displayed an upturned thumb. He peeked around the corner.

A large skylight in the roof poured moonlight down into the warehouse. More shelving units were set out in a ring around the building's outer perimeter, blocking any external view of an open central area. A high gantry stood to one end of the space with a ladder leading up. Beneath was a desk, a series of filing cabinets, and a large, wooden-framed blackboard. But it was the centre of the floor that grabbed his attention. Ducking back, he regarded Merry with crumpled eyebrows.

"What is it?" she whispered.

"I have no idea."

Merry leaned around Alan to spy beyond. Between moonlight and street light, she saw what had confused him. At the warehouse's centre, a massive pile of mattresses had been laid, five thick and at least four to a side.

"You think Moore was practicing his high-wire act?" Alan whispered.

Merry *humphed* and moved out into the warehouse.

With confidence that comes only from practice, they separated. Merry circled the mattresses, trying to peer on top, poking between. Alan headed for the filing cabinets and started opening one drawer after another using the tip of his revolver and peering inside.

"Empty," he called out. "And the blackboard's been rubbed. Looks like Moore got rid of whatever he was working on after he killed Harrison. You think he did a runner?"

"Kind of. But we'll not be catching him where he's gone," Merry called back.

Alan made his way over to where Merry crouched beside a corpse.

Dressed in shirt and braces, his face had taken the brunt of the beating, his forearms and hands swollen and purple.

"That's not a fall," Alan said, looking up at the gantry above. "This fellow was beaten and tried to defend himself. That means…"

"Harrison didn't kill him. He wasn't the beating type. One bullet, if absolutely necessary."

"What's betting this is the engineer? And there's a third person involved."

Merry rifled through the corpse's pockets. "Aha." She held up a small black book, gold embossed with *'1862'*. Sitting on the ground beside the late engineer, she flicked through the pages.

"June 10th is marked as 'USMRD'. And he definitely wasn't planning on dying because he had plans for the theatre this weekend."

"Theatre? He probably killed himself to get out of it," Alan sniffed.

Merry rolled her eyes. "Not everyone is you, Alan. Thank God."

"Charming. Why do I get the feeling that Rook missed something out of the mission brief?"

"Because he always bloody does."

"Here, what's that there?"

Nestled far back against the warehouse wall, partly obscured by the high shelves, was a workstation. Gouges and dents decorated the wooden surface. Tools hung in carefully outlined spaces on the back wall. An unused roll of drafting paper was propped in one corner.

"You know what I can't help but notice?" Alan tapped the workstation with his fingertip. "There's nothing here. No materials. No boxes of spare screws or bits of string. Nothing."

"Bugger all," Merry agreed. "Someone cleaned up."

"And cleaned Harrison up as well. No witnesses."

That was when the sky fell in.

With a crash of crystal cymbals, the skylight turned to splinters of falling, razor sharp moonlight.

Alan dived one way, Merry the other, hitting the ground with arms thrown over heads as shattered glass rained down on them.

"Unlucky, my friends," a voice called down to them in a southern state drawl. "If you'd been just a little dumber, I could have let you live."

Alan rolled to the left, using the momentum to draw his revolver and bring it to bear in one fluid motion. But, at the end of the draw, he paused. Because he wasn't entirely sure what he was aiming at.

Hovering in the vault of the warehouse was a man, of that he was sure. But it was the hooded suit made from overlapping leather scales, the glowing yellow goggle lenses, boots like metal claws that clicked open and closed, and the impressive span of the mechanical wings that made Alan pause for thought. But, for Alan, thinking never lasted long. He fired off a volley, bullets hitting the flying suit's harness, ricocheting from the wings. For all the good it did, he might as well have missed.

The owl-ish arrival chuckled. "You couldn't hit a barn on the broadside, boy."

Alan fumbled to his feet, half scuttling forward toward the cover of the nearest shelves, but his assailant was swooping. He heard it, now… the whir of a motor, the suck and squall of high-pressure air. Something was keeping that thing aloft. He planned on smashing it.

Alan's back lit up with pain and he smashed into the

ground, face-first. He tried to draw a breath but his lungs had no room to expand. He tried to roll but the weight pressing him down was too great. One shard of pain lanced through his shoulder blades, the other down by his hips. Even the spinal support of his armoured waistcoat groaned. He coughed, gasped, drew in a tease of breath that wasn't enough. His palms hit the ground, biceps flared with strain, boots hitting the floor as he struggled. He'd been suffocated before, nearly drowned a few times, and so, when the inky spots began to draw in around his vision, there was no surprise, only fear, and anger.

Shpang.

Air rushed into the vacuum of his lungs. He rolled on reflex, his body throwing up every flag of pain it had. Despite the agonising semaphore, he rolled to his knees, fought to get to his feet.

Merry stood between him and the owlman, a stool raised over her shoulder. The owlman was reeling around, regaining hasty control of his metallic wings, fighting into the air. He snarled, spitting curses that they didn't hear.

"He's going to bolt," Alan said.

"I don't think so. I think he's got a job to do."

"Yeah, well so do we." Alan realised that, despite the pain, he was chuckling to himself. He looked at Merry, and saw a matching grin on her face. "Split!"

Merry spun in a tight arc, scything the stool through the air toward her opponent. With a whir of turbine, her opponent dropped a few inches and rolled, the stool missing by an inch.

"Nice try, girlie," he jeered as he watched Merry dart back toward the workstation. She grabbed a hammer from the display and lobbed it over arm. The villain let out a cry of pain as it gave him a glancing blow on his temple, enough to draw blood, enough to distract him from the wooden mallet that came next, slamming into his chest.

Merry was circling the mattresses now, moving back toward the desk and cabinets. She was unarmed. He swooped, feet first. Merry fell behind the desk as he slammed into it, metallic talons rending, smashing the wood and leaving the desk a useless pile of splinters.

"What're you gonna do now, girlie?" he growled.

"Nothing. It's his turn."

"Here, birdy birdy," Alan sang out.

Snapping his head around, their opponent had just enough to time to gasp as Alan fell from the gantry above, limbs spread wide and grinning like a maniac. Alan crashed into him bodily, arms and legs finding purchase wherever they could in an off-kilter grapple. A whoomph of hot air blasted Merry backward as Privateer and villain rocketed upward. The wings curling in as the villain tried to strike at Alan only sent them spiralling upward in a helix of confusion and panic. Merry screamed something about holding on, or possibly letting go, but Alan was screaming too loud about whether he should hang on or let go to hear her.

The villain must have gotten an idea because he threw out his arms, extending the wings, and, with a neat barrel roll, they were inches from the ceiling. Alan let out a groan through gritted teeth as his back scraped painfully along an exposed girder, his waistcoat taking some of the brunt but not enough. The villain chuckled, so Alan risked letting go with one hand to punch the bastard in the temple. With a cry of pain, they villain shot them skyward again.

What remained of the skylight shattered. Merry stared upward, mouth open, as Alan's scream grew distant, until there was nothing left but the tinkle of shards on concrete.

"Oh bugger," she said.

Craning her neck, she saw only stars and the faint glow of a cloud-covered moon through the skyward window.

She was fighting her way to her feet when she heard another sound. Growing louder. Fast.

"...aaaaaaaaaaaaaaaaaaaaaaaaaaaargh."

She ducked just as a screaming comet plummeted into the warehouse, slamming into the mattresses with a cough of dust and debris.

And silence.

Merry's shallow breath rasped in and out of her. She tried to speak, to say a name, but her throat couldn't even squeak. If anyone was shouting her, she wouldn't hear it; her ears were filled with the pounding of her own pulse. She got up, slowly, and moved closer. The mattress pile was too high for her to peer over, and something inside her didn't want to climb up to see. She swallowed, finally, and managed a whisper.

"Alan?"

She jumped back as the mattresses folded toward her with a groan and spat out a mass of tangled clothing. Alan hit the concrete, not even bothering to cushion his fall. He didn't bother to open his eyes either, but one hand quested out to his side, finding the firm ground, and patted it like an old friend.

"If you ever…" He coughed, and tried again. "…have to knock out the flying man you're riding, make sure you're closer to the ground."

Merry let out a bark of laughter, dropping into a crouch beside him. "I'll bear that in mind."

He nodded, eyes still closed, as she absent-mindedly picked broken glass off his clothes, plucking one piece straight out of his cheek.

"Ow."

"Oh shush."

"Flying men. I'll be damned," Alan said.

"Probably," Merry quipped.

He tried to shake his head but instantly regretted it as his brain rattled around inside and the pounding started all over again. Instead, he gave her a wan smile as his fingers searched toward the pair of small stitches in his cheek for the hundredth time that afternoon.

"Don't pick it."

"Who knew I'd be thirty before I found my mother, and she'd be younger than me," he retorted, but stopped anyway. Reaching for the scotch glass on the bar, he downed it, then took Merry's and polished that off as well.

"So, Harrison was supposed to steal the plans. Only, when he got there, the other Privateer had stolen it already and killed the engineer," Merry said.

"Sounds about right. But now it's gone. Job done. Although maybe not in the way Rook would have wanted."

"Thank God. You can be sure that whoever wants a machine to make flying men isn't planning on starting a courier service. Poor Harrison, caught up in the middle of all that."

"That about sums it all up," Alan said, holding a hand up to the barman for another round. "Except for USMRD. We still don't know what that is."

A deep American accent had them both turning in their stools.

"United States Military Research Division." In a fine black suit and necktie, the new arrival gave them a broad smile. "We're a new branch created under the orders of President Lincoln for developing new technology, primarily to help with the war efforts, but mostly for the betterment of mankind."

Alan and Merry exchanged a glance, and turned back toward the bar.

"That explains that, then," Alan muttered.

But the agent wasn't done. He sidled over, setting his elbow on the bar beside Merry.

"I don't suppose either of you know what happened to

that suit? Or the plans? An invention like that could turn the civil war heavily in our favour."

"I broke it," Alan said.

"He does that," Merry added.

"And where, exactly, did you leave it?"

Alan turned to his partner, a quizzical look on his face. "Where did we leave it, Merry?"

She shrugged. "I forget."

The suit's mouth tightened into a pale line.

"Is that right?" he growled.

"Things rarely are," Alan said.

With an audible growl, the suit made to leave, but shot a glance back at them as he reached the door.

"You certainly know how to make enemies, Mr Shaw. It'd be a shame if any of them found you."

And he was gone.

There was a beat, before Merry asked, "Was that a threat?"

"Not a very good one," Alan said. "Barkeep… another round, please."

About Craig Hallam

Craig Hallam is an author whose works span all corners of fantasy, sci-fi and horror. Since his debut in the British Fantasy Society journal in 2008, his tales have nestled twixt the pages of magazines and anthologies the world over. His gothic fantasy novel, Greaveburn, steampunk trilogy The Adventures of Alan Shaw, and the dark short stories of Not Before Bed have filled the imaginations of geeks, niche and alternative readers with their character-driven style and unusual plots.

•

Also by Craig Hallam

Greaveburn
Not Before Bed
The Adventures of Alan Shaw
Old Haunts (The Adventures of Alan Shaw 2)

Find out more at craighallam.wordpress.com

TAYLORSON
A THIEVES' GUILD STORY

C.G. HATTON

A single spotlight breaks the darkness of the small cell. The figure sitting there blinks, shields his eyes and squints up, right at us as if he knows we're here, watching from the observation deck.

She leans forward and watches as another figure enters the cell, setting a glass of water down in front of him and sitting opposite.

"How are you feeling?" the newcomer says. "Ready for the debrief?"

The soldier sits up straighter.

"Name, rank, unit. Let's start there. For the record."

He looks wary. Not surprising.

"It's alright. Let me start. This is debrief 907/1-1/K. Code AlphaTenDesertZulu."

It's a legitimate code. No reason for him to doubt it.

His shoulders relax a notch. He reaches for the water with his left hand and takes a sip, another glance upwards.

"Go ahead."

"Taylorson." His voice is quiet. "Corporal. JU."

"Good. Now tell me what happened on Kheris."

He stiffens again. "I already…"

"We know that you didn't include everything in your official report, Corporal Taylorson. We want to know what really happened in there."

"We were sent into an alien ship. I lost half my team. What else do you want me to say?"

"Just the truth, Corporal. That's all I'm asking."

•

We flew in low over the colony. It wasn't a combat drop so the blast shutters were up and we could see the flames and the smoke as we approached the city. We all knew what was going on. We've all done tours of Kheris. It's a shit mining colony in the back of the Between that no one ever wants to be posted to. The uprising has been on the cards for years. I was surprised it had taken this long for it to kick off again.

We'd been told we were on a standard recon. An Aries corporation deep spacer that had crashed there. Aries is high priority, at the forefront of the Wintran Coalition's weapons development, everyone knows that, so any opportunity to get inside one of their ships… Only some other Wintran corp had got to it first, United Metals, they reckoned. Someone said the Kheris resistance had jumped at the chance to attack the Imperial garrison because UM had turned up in force. Exactly what an under-manned, under-resourced, hot and dusty shit-hole of an Imperial outpost needed – flash Wintran corporations arming and inciting the local freedom fighters. I don't know. But when the entire colony erupted into outright rebellion, Earth sent in reinforcements, UM pulled out, and we were sent in to recce what was left of the crashed ship. It was only once we landed out in the desert that they told us why they wanted us.

We stood there in the blazing heat and higher than Earth standard gravity of the Kheris wilderness and stared at the crumpled hull of the deep spacer. It was mostly intact. Didn't look like any kind of ship I was familiar with. Not just that it was big, most deep spacers are, just that it looked wrong somehow. Not any spec I recognised. No insignia. No identifying plates or marks at all.

It must have managed some kind of controlled descent but it had crashed into some processing facility or ore refinery, mangled pipes and gantries all that was left of it, debris strewn in a radius around it, all burned black, twisted metal reflecting in the too-bright sun.

Part of the ship was buried deep. The hurried pre-op briefing had mentioned natural subterranean tunnels as well as the mines and it looked like the impact had pushed well below the surface. Some of the trashed refinery towers were still spewing yellow-tinged steam that was winding up into the brilliant blue of the sky, probably the cause of the acidic tang in the air that was catching at the back of my throat and making me feel nauseous. That or just the fact we were on Kheris.

One of the garrison's sub-commanders met us, climbing out of a battered jeep, a Major who looked like he hadn't slept in a week. He didn't bother with any pleasantries. "Whatever they've told you, that's only half the story," he said. "You see that line?" The guy pointed at the desert floor.

It stretched in a perfect circle all the way around the crash site, black scorched earth inside, bright red sand on the other, our side, beneath our boots. The remains of some kind of cordon with guard positions were evident our side of the line, way out behind us, huge chunks of wreckage lying scattered all around. But everything inside that perimeter was black.

He rubbed his temples like he had a headache. "Night of the crash we sent search and rescue teams. Full emergency response. As soon as they got in close, some kind of energy weapon fired from the ship. Perfect radius all round. Took out all of them."

That explained why they wanted to send us in there, not just JU, the two best covert black-ops teams the JU currently had in theatre. Alpha – me, Dixon, Blue and Kobe. Bravo – Narita and his guys.

Dixon glanced at me with that gleam in his eye and sent privately, Senson to Senson, direct, tight wire comm through the implants embedded in our necks, "What did I tell you?"

Blue was our medic. I could see in his eyes that he was tracking through all the possible scenarios. "No survivors?"

"Only one," the Major said. "And only just. Some street kid from the city that was stupid enough to follow them out here. We found him under some wreckage. Kid didn't know what had happened."

Kobes just said, "Shit," hefting her rifle and taking a step forward, peering at it as if she could see back in time if she got closer.

I didn't want to get any closer. I don't know if it was the heat or the fumes making me feel so sick, but ever since we'd touched down I'd felt like crap.

"So Aries were carrying something that no one Winter-side wanted to fall into our hands?" she said. Sergeant Kobe was squad leader for our team. She was the one that had a way of seeing beyond the obvious that had kept us alive too many times to count.

The Major shrugged. "We don't even know if it is an Aries vessel. That's just local rumour. Whatever happened, UM beat us all to it. Weird thing is we can't scan it. If they've developed tech that shields against close range this effectively, we need to know."

"And the weapon?" Narita said, blunt, scuffing his toe across the line, mixing the black dust with the red dirt, before looking up. "Nothing happen when UM was here?"

Narita, Bravo team squad leader and Op 2IC. They were our back up and tech specialists. We were the ice team, they were the brains. We made a helluva combination when we doubled up. His boots blurred as I stared at them, a burning headache starting to nag behind my eyeballs.

"No," the Major said. "Not anything we could see. We just need you to go in there and clear it for the clean up crews. That's it. You need full haz suits. The ship is mostly intact, but it crashed through into the caverns. Whole place is riddled with them. And renowned for toxic gas. Don't take any risks. Document everything. Make sure UM didn't leave any nasty surprises behind for us and get out."

"Roger that," Kobe said. She turned to look at me, piercing me with that stare she has, as if she'd just noticed I wasn't paying attention. "Taylorson, get your shit together. You're on point."

•

UM had torn a hole in the hull, ripped it open from the top and set up scaffolding heading down into its depths. I knew as soon as I ducked down inside that it wasn't Aries or UM.

Plan was to leave Bravo to recce the upper deck and we'd call them if we found anything that needed more tech smarts than us grunts could handle, but as soon as we went in, we knew it was going to be trouble.

I led the way down, gun up, sensors going haywire, right from the off. It was dark, just the beams from our helmet lights and rifle torches giving any illumination. For a ship that had been stranded for days in the middle of one of the galaxy's driest deserts, it was damp inside. Humid. Bio-readings off the scale. I find haz suits cumbersome, restrictive, especially in high gravity, more so if you're expecting trouble, but I have to admit, right then I was glad I was tucked up safely inside it. Even so, my skin was crawling.

"Anyone else feel weird?" I transmitted.

There was no reply.

For a split second it felt like I was down there alone. I spun round, scanning back over with the flashlights, grip firm on the rifle. The team were right there. I tapped the side of my helmet and got a shake of the hand from Dixon, fingers slicing in a negative then opening in a question.

"Rep… that las… bud," he sent.

Intermittent comms.

Great. As if it wasn't freaky enough.

"Does anyone else feel weird?" I said again.

"What i… not weird abou… …is, Taylorson?" Kobe sent through the Senson rather than the suits, even then every other word breaking up. "Get your a… down there."

I stepped off the UM platform into the ship and pressed my hand against the bulkhead. It was smooth, hot according to the readings I was getting. My VHUD was scrolling stats, infrared, thermal, scanning for energy spikes, lifesigns, chemical signatures. It was going wild.

I signalled the others to follow, taking up watch as Blue knelt and dragged his gloved hand across the deck. I couldn't see what it was that had caught his attention but he held his hand up, pulling a quizzical face inside his helmet, and scraped some more off into a sample jar that he dropped into a pouch. He gestured Kobe to get close and the two of them talked direct, helmets touching. I kept position, rifle aimed ahead of us, Dixon covering the opposite direction, and waited, glancing back and seeing that Kobe wasn't impressed with whatever she was hearing.

I was starting to feel more than nauseous. I was secure inside a haz suit and something was pulling my stomach into a knot. You have to understand… we're JU. We don't fear anything. We're trained to not fear anything. It's programmed and conditioned into us. And beyond that, it's inherent. You don't get to be JU if you let the fear get to you. You want to know some of the places I've been? I was at Derren Bay, for Christ's sake. In the middle of the shit at Derren Bay and I didn't even break a sweat. Never, ever, anything like that damned ship on Kheris.

There was a kind of ominous edge like you get right before the kind of thunderstorm that has a lightning strike with your name on it. Even inside the suit, my skin felt like a million tiny iron filings were dancing on every inch of it to the tune of a crazed magnet. I wanted to tear the suit off and run, run as far from that damned ship as possible.

But I'm JU. So I stood there, on watch, finger on the trigger, every sense on alert, stats flashing past my eyes, and watched Kobe move to Narita.

When it was my turn, she bumped helmets and said, clear and downright blunt, "We're all feeling it."

I glanced at Dixon, dubious.

He looked bored, scratching at the smooth clear surface of the bulkhead with the butt of his rifle.

"Okay, not Dixon," she conceded. "Probably because the ape is too thick skulled to realise it, but me and Blue, we are too, and Narita, we can all feel it. It's not just you. This is hinky as hell. Bravo is going to stay here on the upper decks so we can keep in touch with the outside. We need to wind it down, do the job and get out of here."

I nodded. Glad it wasn't just me losing my shit. It was like a dark weight pressing on my soul. And it wasn't just the high gravity, the scale of the ship was off, the corridor we were in too wide, doors up ahead that were a scale too big somehow… and there was a hum to the air pressure in there that I could feel, even through the suit.

"Alpha, we stay together," she said out loud to everyone, voice electronically enhanced through the suit. "We run a standard sweep and we get the hell out. You with me?"

I nodded again. Damn right.

We worked our way down through the ship, having to use grapples in places, feeling like mice in the giant's lair. We ran a textbook close quarters, high risk, search and eliminate, setting motion captures and a sensor array at each junction, a wireframe map of the interior growing as we progressed. These ops were always tense, not knowing what could be around the next corner, but there was something about that ship that got worse the deeper we got. I had a humming vibration in my head that was increasing by a magnitude with each level, every instinct I had screaming at me to get out.

The ship had been stripped clean, wires and cables lying limp where equipment had been torn out. Just an occasional cracked fragment of screen or twisted edge of black conduit. UM had taken everything substantial.

"Taylorson…?"

Kobe had hold of my arm and was turning me before I realised I'd frozen, shoulder to shoulder with Blue, both of us staring through a doorway into a round chamber that was lined with a row of smooth black benches around a sunken floor. It looked like an amphitheatre. Some kind of council chamber. Way too big for any human to sit on. I was struggling to breathe, the pressure against my chest increasing and unease dragging my stomach into a hollow pit.

"I'm good." I wasn't. I wanted to say I wanted out. I wanted to scream and run right out of there like it was on fire. But the JU shrinks are very good at what they do. So I didn't run, no matter how much my gut was telling me to. "Kobes, this isn't just hinky."

Dixon had his rifle up, scanning his flashlight beam around the chamber. "It's not freaking human," he muttered, saying what we were all thinking.

I'd run ops before where my instinct to get out had saved our asses. This wasn't that. It was dread, deep down, a dark knot of impending, dire doom. Not just fear but paralysing irrational fear.

I wasn't the only one. I could see it in their faces.

"Whatever it is," Kobe said, "we have a job to do. Stop gawping, people. Let's get this done. I have a cold beer and a card game waiting for me."

I had to force myself to move, taking point again, heading down steps that were too big, almost jumping down each one, reaching a new deck level and feeling a palpable change in the environment. It might even have been deep enough to be underground, in that part of the ship that had crashed through to the caverns beneath the processing plant.

I took one step out and a shudder ran through my suit, stats plummeting, air gauge hitting red, batteries draining visibly fast. Shit.

•

I turned, held up my hand and yelled, "Wait. Don't come down here. Shit, I…"

…had no idea if they could hear me. I was on one knee before I realised I was falling, out of air, out of power. In an instant. The suit was suffocating me. I couldn't breathe. Oxygen at zero. That fast. I knew I shouldn't but I couldn't help grasping at the clasps, trying to tear the suit off with trembling hands that had no strength.

I started to keel over, arms dropping.

Someone was at my side in an instant, Kobe, grabbing the helmet and pulling it away. I gasped a lungful of hot and humid air that made me gag but it was air. Teeming with god knows what but it was air.

Kobe sagged beside me, same thing happening to her, and it took us both, scrambling against the clasps to free her.

We sat there in the dark, sucking in air that made us both cough, the only illumination a narrow stretch of deck lit up by the tac-lights on the rifles lying where we'd dropped them.

I bumped against her. "I thought I said don't come down here. Didn't you hear me?"

She thumped me. "God, Spud, I thought you'd snuffed it. Shit. What the hell was that?" She leaned forward and shouted, "Dixie, we could do with a torch down here."

They threw two torches and a medikit down to us, and we ditched the suits, stripping off to fatigues and kitting back up, strapping on belts and holsters.

I grabbed my rifle and stood, its beam flashing across the pile of abandoned haz gear. A green light caught my eye, the external oxy gauge on my suit. It still showed 87% full. I knelt and checked battery power, 93%, muttering, "This is weird."

Kobe grabbed hers. "What the hell?"

"We didn't imagine it," I said. "I was suffocating. I could feel it."

She shoved her suit away with disgust. "Well whatever the hell just happened, we're contaminated now. No point putting the haz back on. Let's just get this done." She shone her torch in my face. The beam was fading already. "You okay?"

I nodded. "Never felt better." I kept my torch switched

off, for what difference that might make. I held up one hand and turned it. "Don't seem to be melting or anything."

Kobe grinned. "If your skin starts dropping off your ugly mug, Taylorson, it'll be a freaking improvement. Now move your ass before I kick it."

We moved out. The adrenaline rush from almost dying seemed to have countered the gut churning fear that had been building, but not completely. A deep dread was still lurking, that no amount of bullshit banter could hide. It peaked again as we entered a massive chamber and cast the beam of light onto a cell in its centre, a huge round tube stretching floor to ceiling that looked like a containment facility. Or at least it had been.

The clear panels of the cell walls were shattered and broken, ripped apart, claw marks scratched deep, thick chains lying piled on the floor, whatever had been held in there gone. It reeked of blood, a dank, leafmold stench heavy in the stale air.

Kobe turned slowly, sending the beam of light across charred and blackened bulkheads. Benches around the edges of the chamber looked like they'd held cabinets, racks of bottles, jars, petri dishes, test tubes, intricate scientific or medical equipment, lying smashed and burnt.

She glanced back at me, nose wrinkling. "What the hell was in there?"

I set the sensor, activated it and watched it die down to red in seconds.

"Dixon, Blue..." I tried sending through the Senson. "You getting any of this?"

No reply.

"We need to go," Kobe muttered.

I caught a glimpse of something dark in the corner of my eye, a flash of shadow moving fast.

There was something alive down there... and I swear, it was that thing that was causing the fear. You wanted to know what I didn't include in my report? The closer we got to it, the worse that hideous, ominous dread became. But I know how crazy that sounds.

I spun, gun up. "Kobes...?"

She was angling round, her gun up and pointing in a vector that intercepted mine. "What have you got, Taylorson?"

I took a step forward, keeping the rifle aimed. "I saw something. I don't know what, but there's something in here."

"The thing that was in that cell?"

I had no idea but I knew it was hostile and I knew it wanted us gone. UM must have had a freaking field day working down here in the midst of this. If any of the cold-hearted bastards had noticed it.

It felt like we were being pushed away, the way magnets repel. I'd never felt anything like it, especially when it started to ramp up, like the rumble of drop ship engines when they're gearing up for a fast evac. It reverberated in my chest even though I couldn't hear anything.

She was right, we needed to go. But at the same time,

there was some stubborn, twisted, self-destructive part of me that wanted to reject that instinct as not mine. To move forward rather than run away. Like I knew it wasn't natural, that we were being manipulated.

"Taylorson… c'mon, Spud, talk to me."

Kobe was at ninety degrees to me.

We had it split. It could attack her or it could attack me. Or maybe it could fire out a ripple of whatever the hell it had used to take out the rescue team, and take out both of us. Hell. Take us all out.

JU conditioning kicked in again, fear being rerouted through different pathways in the brain to become hate, anger, a desire to destroy and dominate. Did you know there's a lump of wall in the JU training barracks on Hayes Prime, a bit of masonry recovered from a rogue colony that needed to be re-educated, that stands like a memorial with the motto, 'There is nothing to fear but fear itself'. Underneath some smart ass had scrawled 'and the JU'. Yeah, too right. We're all fun and games, whatever the hell you throw at us.

"We need to find it," I muttered.

It escalated again, that dreadful oppressive weight becoming an unbearable physical pressure inside my head.

I wanted to turn and run but something made me step forward. Another flash of moving shadow caught my eye.

I turned fast, gun up, finger twitching on the trigger and almost firing as two figures stepped into the chamber, their own guns up and aiming at us. My stomach flipped for a second, Kobe was reacting the same, and I don't know what stopped us from firing but it was Dixon who yelled first, lowering the gun and raising his hand.

"Holy shit, people, it's us, calm the hell down. Why did you take off your freaking suits?"

•

Blue said, more calm, moving round, his gun still up, "What you got down here?"

"Taylorson saw something," Kobe said, tracking her own aim around the walls.

Whatever I'd spotted had gone.

I kept my gun up.

Blue edged towards the cell, helmet lights sending the shadows into frenzy. "Why did you take off your suits?"

"They malfunctioned."

He looked at her. "Kobes, the suits you left back there are fine. All stats fine. All levels fine. There was nothing wrong with them."

"We were suffocating, Blue. I know when a damned suit malfunctions. I don't care what the gauges say now." She glared round at us. "Dixon, Taylorson, get over there and give me eyes on those two corridors. We still have a job to do. Let's do it and get the hell out. If there's something down here, let's find it. Taylorson, you still got the heebie-jeebies?"

"I'm good." I was lying. It was getting worse again. And I was damned if I'd imagined what had happened with the suit. A shadow flitted across my vision and shot down the corridor away from us. "Kobe..." I tracked it with my rifle, never really seeing it, and was following it before I realised I was, Kobe cursing and moving to my right, covering me.

It vanished as fast as it appeared into the darkness of a corridor that headed down, bulkheads partially caved in, the deck uneven. The beam from my weapon's tac-light flickered, making the shadows increase, eerie dancing shapes that evaporated whenever I tried to look at them direct.

I didn't stop, aware that Kobe was behind me, glancing back to see Blue and Dixon walking half backwards, covering our asses as we got deeper into the crashed ship.

We dropped down another level and the damage got worse, the heat more oppressive. Sweat was trickling down my ribs. My head was pounding, the thrumming noise building, that dank stench in the air getting stronger. I was still on point, slipping a couple of times as deck panels shifted beneath my feet, still chasing wraiths.

Kobe called out, "Taylorson, wait up. Dixon, you getting anything on sensors?"

"Affirmative on that. There's some kind of energy reading up ahead. You want an array?"

I had no idea why his sensors were working and mine were trashed but I stopped and took up position, watching the darkness stretching out ahead of us, hoping his damned sensors would give us some intel to work off.

Blue walked up beside me, rifle up, aiming down the passageway. "You okay?" he said casually in that way medics have right before they say your stats are shit.

"I'm good," I said again.

"Your stats are shit. What's wrong?"

"We're on a freaking alien ship, Blue. What's not wrong?" I didn't look at him, shifting my weight to adjust the angle I had and keeping my eyes on the darkness for what good it was doing. "I'm just too hot. I'd forgotten how shit Kheris is. I'll be…" The thrum against my chest spiked, vicious, internal temperature rising so fast I couldn't catch my breath. I started to turn. Dixon was ramping up the array. "Shit… Dixie, don't…"

He initiated the sensors.

I was moving before I could think, bundling into him and shoving him out of the way as a blast of energy sparked between each one like a lightning flash.

Light flared so bright I couldn't see.

The pressure in my lungs peaked. I was thrown backwards. And I plunged into a nightmare of heat and pain and dark so dense I didn't know if I had my eyes open or closed.

I felt a cold sting against my neck, two more in fast succession. I blinked. Still dark.

"…any time you like, Spud…"

Dixon.

Another voice echoed from far away. "Whole ship has split open down here. I'm coming back up. Is he going to be good to move?"

Kobe. Maybe.

There was a tap against my cheek.

I tried to move, respond, anything and obviously failed as Dixon yelled back, his voice sending sparks flaring behind my eyes, "Negative. Gonna have to carry sleeping beauty out of here unless you wanna give him a pop of insanity."

"I… awake," I managed to mumble. "What…?"

"Scratch that," Dixon yelled, needle-sharp spikes driving into my eyeballs at each word, "there's life in the Spud-bunny yet. Let's go."

"Roger that," she shouted back. "I just need to… Wait. Give me a minute."

It went quiet.

Eerily quiet.

I swallowed, throat parched, and managed to say, "What happened?"

"Sensor array exploded. Deck gave out. We're about two levels down from where we were. Kobe dropped another two. She's just trying to find a way up then we're getting the hell out of here."

I tried to move and thought better of it.

"I'm gonna get up top," Dixon said, "get Bravo to call in a medevac, then we ride the hell outta here and share out those beers." He raised his torch to shine its beam into his face. He grinned. He wasn't wearing his suit anymore either. Blood was streaming trails down his cheek. "If there's any damned aliens in here, Delta can come round 'em up." He dropped the grin. It wasn't often Dixon got serious. "Cheers, Spud."

He squeezed my shoulder and moved away.

I was struggling to breathe.

Blue took his place, popping more shots into my neck. "How did you know the array was going to blow?"

"Honestly?" I croaked. "If I tell you I felt it, are you gonna send me to the psychs?"

"Well, whatever it was, you just saved Dixon's life. The numbskull is too stubborn to realise he has a concussion. Kobe broke her arm but she's fine. You, Spud, are the lucky recipient of one broken leg and a chunk of wreckage embedded just about..."

He didn't touch me but even just a brush of his fingers sent a new wave of agony washing through my chest, even through the numb heat I knew was a trauma patch.

"I need to get this out," he said, "and we need you walking. How's your head now?"

"Sore."

"How's the...?" He didn't say heebie-jeebies but he didn't need to.

I squinted at him and closed my eyes, listening in as Dixon exchanged shouts with Kobe. It was still bad enough that I didn't want to think.

"Just do it," I muttered.

We didn't have time to mess about.

He peeled back the trauma patch. There was a hot scraping, spiking pain, then heat flared again as he pressed the patch back down. I almost faded back under but Kobe started shouting again and I caught, "...something down here..." and my stomach turned.

•

"Tell her to get out of there."

"We're all getting out of here. I need to strap your leg."

"Do it, and tell Kobe to get out of there."

I heard her shout again. "Guys, you need to see this. Blue, we can't leave without this. Get down here. We need samples. Is Taylorson good to go?"

There was a tug, something clamped tight around my thigh, and I lost track of everything for a moment. I'd broken my leg before, twice, had to walk on it both times to get out of the shit. It was going to be bad but all I could think was that I wanted Kobe away from whatever it was down there.

"Help me sit up," I muttered and blinked as Blue pulled on my arm and pulled me up, helping me settle with my back against the bulkhead, one leg stretched out in front of me, the other knee drawn up. "Where's my rifle?" The ominous pressure of dread was overpowering. I couldn't help shivering.

He nestled it into my arms, the weight of it welcome as I embraced it and rested a shaky finger against the trigger guard.

He squeezed my shoulder. "You good?"

"I'm good. Go. Get her out of there, Blue. Whatever it is, we need more firepower than we have."

"We know. Dixie's already calling in reinforcements. Hold tight, yeah?"

I didn't have much choice. Being incapacitated in the middle of a mission sucks. Being incapacitated at the bottom of a crashed alien ship with the threat level skyrocketing is something else.

He left me and I sat there, rifle resting on my good knee, trying to breathe without wheezing and stay awake enough to keep watch. Though what I'd do if anything came at me, I had no freaking idea. Every slight creak and groan of metal had me twitching. There was nothing on comms. Nothing on sensors. Sweat was trickling down my back and every muscle was aching, bone deep. Every dark shadow I could see moving was shot through with sparks of bright light.

A couple of times I heard echoes, voices, the pressure in my head building, exponentially. It spiked. Someone screamed and I didn't know if I was imagining it or it was real, but I tried to get up and dark heat swirled in close and fast, vision narrowing to a tunnel. Someone grabbed my arm, one each side, the weight of the rifle vanishing, voices I couldn't make out close by, calm but tense, and as I was hauled to my feet, I recognised Dixon shouting.

"Whatever they're doing, tell them to stop," I mumbled. "It's going to attack again."

I could feel it. Feel the energy sparking.

The shouting echoing up from below got louder.

One of Narita's guys muttered, "That's not our only problem," and yelled, "Kobe, leave it. The damn power plant is about to blow. We have to get out of here now. Kobe, do you copy?"

"What are they doing?"

It was Narita on my right side. "They're collecting

samples but, yes, we're getting the hell out." His voice sounded miles away as he said, "What…?" sounding more faint.

There was screaming, shouts, frantic yells, all far off, unreal.

This wasn't how we operated.

Someone shouted, "Kobe," the words cut off as a shockwave billowed into us, the blast knocking us off our feet.

Echoes reverberated around my head, ringing in my ears. My chest was burning, my leg numb.

Narita was yelling. I couldn't hear Kobe or Blue, but in an instant I was getting dragged up again, and we were moving.

"No." I coughed, spitting dust. "Wait. Where's Kobe?" I tried to look around. "Dixie? Where's Kobe and Blue?"

Narita was talking to someone else. I couldn't follow who.

"Why is the power plant going to blow?"

"I don't know," Narita muttered, hoisting me up and swearing. "C'mon, Taylorson, dammit, move."

Someone appeared at my other side and we started to speed up, as if someone was monitoring a countdown and knew exactly how little time we had.

After an age, we scrambled up and out into the remains of the plant, corrugated sheets lying twisted and broken, pipes hissing that yellow acrid steam. I doubled over and coughed, looking out across the shimmering haze of the desert. There were gunships incoming. I wasn't so far out of it that I didn't know something was wrong.

"They're not ours," I said, struggling to get the words out. "Narita, they're not ours. What's going on?"

"Damned if I know," he muttered, sending through the Senson on an open link, "Command, we need immediate evac. Where are you?" Someone must have replied, something I missed, because he sent, "Negative. Need a go, Command. We're running out of time here."

The hull of the alien ship was glinting, that oppressive weight still clawing at the edges of my mind, competing with the headache.

"Where's Kobe?"

No one answered.

I tried to turn, trying to find my team, and lost my footing as a fresh wave of dread washed over me. I fell to one knee.

Then Dixon was there, swearing at me to move, shouting, trying to drag me up. It was overwhelming. I felt like I was moving through treacle.

There was a downdraft, heat, the roar of engines. Someone grabbed my jacket, hauling me up and into a gunship.

There was a yell of, "Go," and it lifted, the rumble and vibration of the engines sending spikes into my eyeballs.

Someone gave me a shot and that was it.

I woke up in a medical facility.

They told me the blast took out the entire site, the crashed ship, the remains of the facility. Kobe and Blue were still down there with one of Narita's guys when it blew.

I know those gunships that picked us up weren't JU. Am I back with the unit now? Because no one will tell me anything. I haven't seen Dixon since we were picked up a week ago. And no one's even told me what the hell that ship was…

•

A week ago? It hasn't been a week. My god, the poor bastard doesn't know what we've done to him. But from everything we've just heard, it's obvious to everyone standing there on the observation deck that, whatever the hell it was, the ship that crashed on Kheris ten years ago was not Bhenykhn.

I watch as she stands there, stoic, no emotion crossing her face.

This changes everything.

Whichever race or species the ship had belonged to, the Bhenykhn warrior had been their prisoner, not crew.

The soldier sits back, raising his eyes to the window as if defying us to question him further. It's curious to see such emotion, so raw, now, after so many years.

"So Corporal Taylorson is an empath." Drake stares down at him.

"Yes, ma'am. He scores exceptionally high on the gradient."

It should have been in his record but I'm not surprised it isn't. The military might of the Earth Empire, even the exemplary January Unit, has always been notoriously bad at missing the true potential in their people.

"Put him back into cold storage," she says. "I'll keep Corporal Taylorson for later. Right now I want UM. Find me someone that was down there when the alien was still there."

"Yes, ma'am."

"And I want the child that survived."

That might be a problem. "It was just a street kid. According to the Imperial records we salvaged, he was taken into the garrison but…" I hesitate. "…considering what happened, chances that the kid made it out of there alive are negligible."

"If he did, find him. What happened on Kheris ten years ago is now key to the outcome of this war. I want to know what happened. I want to know how that child survived. I want to know why that ship crashed in the first place. If the Bhenykhn have a weakness, it's right there on Kheris." Drake turns to her companion, the one we've all been at such pains to handle with care considering the circumstances. "And trust me," she says, "if you want to survive this war, you want me to be the one to find it – not the damned Thieves' Guild."

About C.G. Hatton

C.G. Hatton is the author of the fast-paced, military science fiction books set in the high-tech Thieves' Guild universe of galactic war and knife-edge intrigue. She has a PhD in geology and a background in journalism, is a regular at comic cons in London and New York, and is currently working on the eighth book in the Thieves' Guild series.

•

Also by C.G. Hatton

Residual Belligerence (Thieves' Guild Book One)
Blatant Disregard (Thieves' Guild Book Two)
Harsh Realities (Thieves' Guild Book Three)
Wilful Defiance (Thieves' Guild Book Four)
Darkest Fears (Thieves' Guild Book Five)

Kheris Burning (Thieves' Guild Origins: LC Book One)
Beyond Redemption (Thieves' Guild Origins: LC Book Two)

Find out more at www.cghatton.com

THE CHEESECAKE DICHOTOMY

A HANNIBAL SMYTH MISADVENTURE

MARK HAYES

I could smell the colour purple and hear the colour green, but I could only see in black and white, except for music, music I could see in all its technicolour wonder. It occurred to me then, as I fumbled with what I hoped was my sabre, that it would have been wiser not to have taken LSD with my breakfast, before fighting a dual.

My opponent in this farcical endeavour, Mr Charles Fortescue-Wright III, currently looked like nothing less than an overstuffed pig, with beady eyes and a snout for a nose. I took some heart from this, as it suggested I wasn't hallucinating too badly. CFW, you see, was beyond doubt an utter pig of a man, and a bit of a prig come to that. It was at his instigation I found myself standing on Hampstead Heath at five in the morning, and for what reason, I hear you ask. What outrage had caused this turn of events, what matter of honour that no gentleman could let slide? An affair of the heart perhaps? The chastity, or lack of such, of a lady? Perhaps, an insult a tad too cutting? Was it some black act of mine? What, indeed, could be the issue of honour between myself and a pig face house-guards lieutenant, with a reedy little voice? For I doubt not you assume that the blame lays with me, even if I, Hannibal Smyth, protest otherwise. I am after all a man with a certain, not entirely respectable, reputation.

Mine is a reputation not entirely undeserved, as I have on occasion mentioned in these memoirs before, however, I may be a lying, rapacious swine, but in these writings to you, dear reader, I seldom lie to further my own advantage or improve the opinion of me you might hold. My dual on that misty Hampstead morning, however, took place some years ago and I was younger then. Thus the reputation I was to earn in later life was yet to cloud my character.

Back then I was merely a young officer in Old Iron Knickers' Royal Air Navy and one not long commissioned. Indeed, at the time I'd yet to set out on the course that would so blacken my later character. While I'll not claim I was a youth of high morals, on this occasion the fault that lay behind this dual was not my own. Indeed when it comes down to it, the fault lay with a slice of cheesecake. That such a thing led to the drawing of swords on a chilly August morning, well it doesn't seem to me that that cheesecake should have led to these just deserts. But I should perhaps explain…

In Soho, just down the road from the little known but highly influential Diogenes club, and the somewhat more well known, some would say infamous, Hellfire club, resides '*The Ins & Outs*'. A club without the dark reputation of the latter or the nefarious intrigues of the former. It takes its name from the prominent signs on its gateposts, and is more correctly known as 'The Naval, Air and Military Club', by no one who has ever frequented it. My own membership of that moderately fine institution is of late somewhat laxed, these days. I suspect I'd be blackballed should I reapply, indeed I suspect even the Hellfire club would blackball me, shortly before they had the peelers drag me away to Bow Street, where I suspect I would find myself blackballed in another, somewhat painful, way. But that is now, then is 'another country' as Hartley would have it, and back then I was a member in good standing.

To an aspiring young officer, looking to further his career, '*The Ins & Outs*' was for me the logical choice. I didn't have the family connections for '*The United Service*' or '*The A&N*,' or any other club for that matter, but '*The Ins & Outs*' was less strict than those older intuitions. Indeed, the club had become even less strict after it moved to a Soho, rather than St James Square at the end of the last century. There was something about that locality, so close to other fine old London institutions, the bars, the bookmakers and other places beginning with a b, that encouraged a more liberal viewpoint. Which is to say it was in spitting distance of London institutions often described in the broadsheets as being of ill repute, and in tabloids like The Times as '*Riotous pits of filth and degradation*', '*Latter-day Sodom and Gomorrah*', and '*A stain on the moral fibre of the nation*' generally just below pictures of ladies in tight corsets, showing a remarkable amount of ankle.

Unsurprisingly, its locality made '*The Ins & Outs*' so popular with younger officers like myself.

Ironically, the other attraction of '*The Ins & Outs*' was it was also one of the few '*Gentlemen's*' clubs in London that allowed for members who weren't in fact gentlemen. By which I don't mean it allowed rogues and villains, though there was a fair share of them among its members, as with any other Gentlemen's club. Rather '*The Ins & Outs*' took applications from those members of Her Royal Clockworkness's armed forces who weren't in fact of the male persuasion. As long as you were an officer in one of the services, it didn't matter if you habitually wore skirts or trousers to work, you could apply for membership. Though by that definition the same could be said of those establishments that maintained a male-only membership, but let's not talk about the Earl of Sunderland.

Suffice to say '*The Ins & Outs*' allowed ladies not only escorted entry to the building, but membership of that fine old intuition itself. Something that marked the club as progressive in the extreme, and progressive liberal attitudes are always an attraction to the youth. Even such hidebound traditionalists as Her Majesty's young officer corps.

Admittedly, after twenty years of this liberal progressiveness policy of cross-gender membership no matter what you had between your legs, '*The Ins & Outs*' female membership numbered two. The first of which had briefly been elected '*Chairman of the Selections Committee*'. This had been just before Brigadier Brendan Fitz-William, a distinguished army officer who had served with no little valour before his retirement, had opted for both surgery and shortening of her name by a single letter. Indeed it was Brenda Fitz-William who put forward the change in membership policy in his brief tenure as COSC, which led to her membership not being called into question after the operation. She was of course removed from office once the transformation was complete, as there was a further motion by the board which read '*It's Chairman, not Chairwoman*', because even for a progressive club like '*The Ins & Outs*' there are some bridges that are too far.

New members joining the club were often disappointed to discover that it wasn't the boiling pot of mixed company they expected. The wives of the sitting selections committee were very firm with their husbands about allowing actual females through selection. For some reason, they considered their husbands' club, which featured among other things two dozen bedrooms for members' use if they were in the city, as an undesirable place for young ladies of the Women's Royal Air-Service officer corps to be frequenting. What with all the recruitment posters on the tube of blonde girls in their uniforms of tightly corseted jackets and skirts several inches above the floor. It was bad enough the club was wedged on Broadwick Street between two bordellos and backed onto a brothel. But the wives certainly didn't want young girls of '*that type*' inside the club itself. As such the only actual female member of the club other than the now septuagenarian Brenda Fitz-William was Warrant Officer Hettie Clarkhurst. A girl no wife could ever disapprove of, no matter how hard they tried.

Hettie Clarkhurst was actually the kind of girl men often enjoy the company of, while never really thinking of them in terms of their gender. She was also something of a force of nature. Our Germanic cousins would have described her as a Valkyrie, of the Wagner operatic, two dirigibles fighting a war against a corset, and a backside closely related to the ponies she used to ride in her youth, with a voice that could shatter the lens on your goggles at fifty paces, kind of way.

She had also, at some point not long after she had got bored with riding the animals her thighs had started to crush, developed a surprising interest for a young lady in mechanics. All the boundless energy that had been consumed in her childhood by the pony club had been transferred to the inner working of steam turbines, engine housings and load bearing pinions (whatever they were). When Hettie wasn't at the club telling jokes bluer than mine, she'd have her sleeves rolled up, and arms black with grease while she de-funked a flue, or stripped down a Rolls 17 venting combinator (again, I don't have a clue).

Let me just lay my cards on the table here. I'm a man

happy to live with the benefits of modern technological marvels, but one without any desire to understand their inner workings. But let's not digress down that particular blind alley…

Warrant Officer Clarkhurst was also the average chief engineer's greatest nightmare. Not because of her gender, I should add, chief engineers tend to be practical men who don't worry much about what was hidden in their officers' trousers. No, she was the average chief engineer's greatest nightmare, because she was an engineering officer who actually knew how things worked, and if it came down to it would roll up her considerable sleeves and start helping out. Worse still, if you told her it would take twenty-four hours to swap out the central cooling feistier (I made that up, so don't ask me what it is), she would ask you why? Because she would know full well it was a two-hour job and she'd hang around to see it was done right. So there was no way you could slope off to the pub for a few hours then enjoy a quiet evening with a bottle of port and a cigar, playing cards with the crew while you chalked up time and a half.

Remarkably, despite this, I never heard a bad word said about her by any engineer who worked under her, and they would curse officers for breathing in their direction normally.

Hettie, or '*Spanners*' as she was known with some affection in the lounge bar of the '*The Ins & Outs*' was, therefore, the kind of girl no wife would ever object to in other words. A girl who was more bloke in their eyes than a broad. She was also, therefore, that rare commodity, a woman who could be your husband's acquaintance who was no threat to the marital harmonies. She was more likely to find a boiler valve assembly interesting than any man, and any man was more likely to ask her how a boiler valve assembly actually worked than for a peck on the cheek. She was as sexually threatening to the wives, as the man who delivered the coal. Such was the logic of the half bulimic military wives who made a competition out of starving themselves in order to fit in corseted ball gowns each year for '*The Ins & Outs*' shindigs, that they couldn't imagine the large woman in the corner laughing with their husbands while smoking a cigar and downing single malts could conceivably be a threat to their marriages.

About this the wives were correct, no one would be leaving their wife or engaging in a long sordid affair with Hettie '*Spanners*' Clarkhurst. What they weren't correct about was why. '*Spanners*', was not, as they doubtless assumed, a woman who was lascivious only for other women. Indeed '*Spanners*' generally found other women nothing but irritations, unless they understood how a flux repeating capacitor worked (nope not a clue). Hettie's affections generally lay with big men with beards who had a working understanding of vent flow dynamics (frankly, wibble). She also considered sex with the same practical eye she considered everything else.

She once told me and several others who were gathered at the bar at one of those shindigs, "It's fine way to relieve tension, I'll give it that much. Get it out of your system if it's making you tense and you can focus on more important things. Oh and have you seen the new reverse compression glandings for tesla loop oxitators… " (I hadn't, and if I had I wouldn't know I had).

As such '*Spanners*' would, maybe once or twice a year, use one of the members' rooms and one of the members, well not to put too fine a point on it, members. If that was, she was of the right frame of mind one evening when she was in town. The '*lucky*' individuals were of course gentlemen to a man. So generally they didn't say a word about what went on within the close walls of a member's room. At least until after their third whiskey the following night, if '*Spanners*' was out of earshot.

I never had the pleasure, if that's the right word, myself. But to a man they described it as an experience they would never forget, more than one adding, '*no matter how hard I try…*' They all had a certain pained expression about them and generally walked funny for a couple of days or more. But Hettie never repeated the exercise with any man twice. Indeed, she seemed to put the whole business out of her mind when next she saw them, save to buy them a double Glenmorangie, and then ask them if they knew anything about the new cross ratchet inverted spindles that were being fitted to the Mark VII Benson's value couplers (not a sausage, but she told me once they were worse than the Mark VI versions and a '*right bugger to snap weld*' (again, wibble)).

Before too long, being '*Spannered*' became something of a rite of passage. By the time I joined '*The Ins &*

Outs' it had almost become legend. But all this led to two distinct facts. The first of which was the wives were both correct about Hettie not being a threat to their marriages, just not for the right reason. Secondly, no club member was ever likely to fall in love with '*Spanners*', she was one of the boys, all be it one of the boys who was also a girl who occasionally '*Spannered*' one of the boys, but she was still one of the boys.

There is, however, an exception to every rule, and in the case of falling for Hettie Clarkhurst, Charles '*Piggie*' Fortescue-Wright III was that exception. For '*Piggie*' was in love with '*Spanners*', though perhaps infatuated is a better word, and everyone knew it. Everyone that is but Hettie. Hettie didn't seem to notice him at all, or tried her best not to. But then if there was ever a man who knew less about the inner workings of mechanical things than I, it was CFW. I doubt he knew one end of a screwdriver from another. His family had people for that kind of thing…

Despite his lovelorn attachment to Hettie, to the best of my knowledge, '*Piggie*' had never been the recipient of a good hard '*spannering*'. Perhaps, if he had, I wouldn't have found myself on Hampstead Heath in the post-dawn light, trying to figure out what the idiot was saying to me while wrestling with my sabre. A sabre which due to the drugs I'd taken an hour or so before had taken on the aspect of a sentient serpent. At least to my perceptions.

If you've ever wrestled with a snake in the pre-dawn light, while neon pink clouds drift through a sky which could have been called tangerine, you would be aware that Lucy may reside in the lower stratosphere with highly compressed carbon atoms, but it's not a fit state to find yourself in when defending someone's honour. Even, that is, if the honour in question is your own, is slightly tarnished and not really something of overwhelming value to anyone. Luckily I wasn't there to defend my honour, but to defend the honour of a woman who wouldn't thank me for doing so, and would probably call me a prat for getting myself involved in the first place.

If that was she wasn't standing on the sidelines, laughing at both of us with the rest of the boys.

But I'm getting ahead of myself. I should perhaps tell the story in its entirety. So let me take you back to the evening before, sometime around four whiskeys, or ten o'clock.

I was, it's fair to say, a tad tipsy at the time. I'd been back in London only a few hours after returning from a two month extended patrol up to Greenland and across to Canada, before coasting down the eastern seaboard of the formerly United States, then back again. It was a routine patrol, which is to say dull as dishwater. We dropped off a few supplies here and there, and picked up a few passengers with the right kind of passports. For the most part, I had my men cleaning gun carriages and playing cards. We didn't even get a stopover in New New York; unseasonal winds had seen us delayed, so we dropped off packages at the British consulate and set off once more. I was starved of entertainment, cards with gun hands and the cheap gin they swill down pales after a while. As such, once I signed off duty for the weekend at the Heathrow towers, I caught a tri-train into the city and headed for my club, to eat, shower and partake of a couple at the bar before moving on to other delights.

There was the usual ribbing one expects when one returns from a long stint aboard ship. The army officers always like to make the odd lewd comment about us naval lads, be it the senior service or those like myself whose ships sail currents of air. I laughed them off and enjoyed the company while a couple of drinks at the bar progressed to several.

Harvey Wigsworth was regaling us all with a tale about a sergeant-major's wife of his acquaintance, which was turning into a long and rather unfortunate tale at that. But his story slipped to the wayside when Hettie Clarkhurst wandered into the bar looking mildly flustered.

I wondered at his hesitation for a moment, not least because Hettie enjoyed a good blue story as much as anyone else in the bar. Then I saw the look on his face was one of disquieting anguish. A sure sign that Harv had likely joined the ranks of the '*Spannered*' while I was away on patrol. I smiled the secret smile of one in the know and did my best to help out the poor lad who clearly felt embarrassed to be caught telling a lewd tale at that particular moment. He clearly would love the subject to be changed quickly…

"And then what happened to the cucumber?" I asked.

Hettie burst out laughing. "Oh, that sounds interesting.

Do tell?" she inquired with a certain lewdness to her own tone, much to Harv's embarrassment.

I'll say this for '*Spanners*', she had a very direct approach to normalising things with someone she had slept with. She wasn't embarrassed in the slightest so they had '*sod all reason to be*', in her opinion. Wigsworth, clearly not agreeing with this, spluttered somewhat. Clearly not yet in that state of normalcy '*Spanners*' dwelt within, he spluttered a little desperate for something to change the subject with. He downed his scotch quickly, spied a tray left over from the evening meals at the far end of the room and he spluttered out what in the end became fateful words for myself.

"Oh I say, does anyone want some cheesecake? There appears to be some left…"

At which point the bar exploded in hilarity.

In our defence we were, most of us at any rate, a little drunk at the time, so this desperate plea for a subject change was possibly the funniest thing anyone could have said. Needless to say Harv's face turned redder than beetroot. Hettie Clarkhurst however amongst her myriad of strange charms is also a kind-hearted soul, and seeing Harv was still in some distress, decided to help him out a tad. Least I suspect this was the reason she said, "Oh actually I wouldn't mind a bit of cheesecake!"

Of course, she was also a large girl who liked cake, so it's possible she was just hungry…

It was at this point in the proceedings Charles '*Piggie*' Fortescue-Wright walked through the door. No doubt just in time to hear her exclamation. Thus my '*good friend*' '*Piggie*' saw the opportunity he'd been waiting for, apparently, for several months. And in a loud voice declared… "Please allow me, Miss Clarkhurst," saying it with lascivious grace.

I tried, and failed, not to find mirth in the way he waddled to the cake stand with undue haste. Presumably to make sure no one else got there before him, and thus prevent him from presenting his prize to '*Spanners*' in person. I didn't try very hard, but I did try. But as the irritating fool bumbled about at the cake stand, I and the rest of my cohort sniggered for a moment, then lost interest swiftly. Though as someone asked, "What did happen to the cucumber anyway?" I noticed out of the corner of my eye that Hettie Clarkhurst had an oddly pained expression on her face and had kept her eyes firmly on Charles at the cake stand.

I was drunk and I'm occasionally a little dim about such things, but I started to suspect there was something I, and everyone else, was missing. I remembered Hettie had looked a tad flustered when she arrived, and found myself wondering about that again. She had entered the bar through the same door that CFW had, only a moment or so before him in fact. That flustered look was unlike her. If there was ever a woman upon whom flustered looked wrong it was '*Spanners*'. The engine room could be on fire, bullets ripping through the walls, blood and bodies everywhere, and I swear Hettie Clarkhurst would just roll up her ample sleeves and get on with the job at hand, whatever that may be. So flustered, well, it just didn't fit. Something had happened that was outside the norm, I realised, and I suspected it had happened in that corridor.

"Look, can we get off the subject of cucumbers?" Harv replied, uncomfortable once more.

"Happily old son, if you just answer the question," someone added, who may have been me...

"Oh for the love of..." Harv started, then pulled up short, his gaze locked on something behind me. He wasn't the only one either, an outbreak of staring had overtaken most everyone.

I turned slowly, to see what spectacle was so intriguing my fellows, and discovered of all things it was CFW down on one knee, holding a plate with a slice of cheesecake on it up to Hettie Clarkhurst. This alone would've begged some surprise, but it was the diamond ring that had been perched in the middle of that slice of cheesecake that was causing the hush that had overtaken the room.

'*Piggie*' was looking up at the object of his desire with something between a pleading expression and ill-advised expectation. I knew the second of those only too well. I may have been accepted in the confines of '*The Ins & Outs*' and had gained a certain social standing as an officer in Her Royal Bavarian sausage eaters Air-Navy. But I was still a product of a social class most of my '*friends*' in the club didn't give a second thought to. While I was tolerated, they seldom actually let me forget who I was, and they all adopted a look of expectation at times. Or perhaps expectation is the wrong word; it wasn't that they expected anything, to expect is to believe even for a moment that there may a possibility of disappointment. Entitlement is the word I should have used. The Fortescue-Wrights of the world do not expect anything; they just assume it is theirs to start with.

Hettie, however, looked incandescent.

I could hazard a guess at why. Within the confines of '*The Ins & Outs*' she had gained a certain degree of acceptance, or for another word, equality. I doubt any of my fellows would understand that. They may not have all hailed from the same social heights as the Fortescue-Wrights of the world, but they were all former public schoolboys. Men of a certain standing. Men of a certain class. Men being the operative word. I may have had little in common with Hettie Clarkhurst, but I understood what it was like to be the fish from the duck pond swimming in the river. '*The Ins & Outs*' may allow female members, much as the world in general allowed ladies to do a great many things, but they were still members of the gentler sex, they still got married and took on their husbands' names. A woman could these days be strong and independent, she could even be considered an equal. Just as long as she was never too strong, or too independent and, well, too equal.

Hettie '*Spanners*' Clarkhurst, in the confines of the club, had until that moment been one of the chaps. But Charles Fortescue-Wright III in that simple and ill-considered act of a proposal had managed to return her to her former status. She was now merely a lady in the eyes of all the chaps in the room. And all those eyes were looking at her just as expectantly as '*Piggie*'s piggy little eyes. After all, it was clear to them, he was doing her an honour just by asking. He was a Fortescue-Wright. His father was Brigadier General Charles Fortescue-Wright II, and as I discovered later, had a barony and owned a large portion of Surrey. He was a world above a mere Clarkhurst in social standing. She would of course therefore accept, and in future would be Mrs Charles Fortescue-Wright III. How, in the eyes of my comrades, could she not?

Only, well, one look into Henrietta Clarkhurst's eyes told me all I needed to know.

I'm not sure what possessed me to intervene at this point. It was an action certainly not going to do me any favours. I could blame an odd feeling of equality I have to the oppressed. Or perhaps I could blame the drink, but it's a poor show when a man's liquor leads them to make a poor decision… Perhaps it just struck me as the gentlemanly thing to do. But if so I've no idea why I was doing it…

All the same, as Hettie just stared at the diamond in front of her, and time stretched out with a pause more pregnant than Queen Sticky Vic in the early years of her reign, I decided someone had to step in and as no one else seemed about to, that someone was me…

"Dashed poor show, Charles old boy. You've dropped something in the cake, man, and made a bally fool of yourself into the bargain," I said, going for belligerent bravado, rather than any more considered approach.

I lent across and plucked the offending item out of the

cheesecake, and pretended to examine it closely. Which in truth I was, not least because I was wondering how much it was worth and if I could find a way to pocket the damn thing. I will say this much for '*Piggie*', he wasn't a cheap swine. I was more than tempted to do a runner with it if I am honest.

Whatever spell the proposal had cast upon the room was now broken as the chaps burst out laughing. In part at my antics and in part at the kneeling Charles, still holding the little china plate with the cheesecake upon it, that expectant look upon his face morphing into anger, rage, mixed with a little bewilderment at this turn of events. The laughter got all the harder as I paraded the ring around the barroom, holding it aloft as if it was a trophy won in fair sportsmanlike fashion.

Most in the room were laughing with me, and at Charles. But importantly, in my view, no one appeared to be laughing at Hettie Clarkhurst. She instead was now smiling and laughing herself, and as Charles remained kneeling, she picked the cheesecake delicately off the plate and walked over to a bar stool, where she promptly perched herself, watched me continue to act the sporting fool and quite deliberately started to consume the cake…

It was all going rather well in fact, with much laughter hilarity, and even the occasional cheer. Right up to the point Charles recovered his wits and focused not on his desire for the hand of dear old '*Spanners*' but the rage burning in his heart, if you will pardon the mellowdrama.

I didn't see the slap coming, as I was just turning in his

direction at the time, or else I'd have ducked beneath it. Instead I took it full on the jaw, lost the ring, which went skittering across the bar-floor, as I stumbled backwards and to the deck. Thus I found myself looking up at an angry pig face house-guards lieutenant. Determined to get his pound of flesh.

"Damn you, Smyth! Damn you back to the gutter. But I'll damn well cut a piece from you first, you swine…" he ranted, or something of that order.

Which brings us back to where we began, on Hampstead Heath at five in the morning. A matter of honour to be settled, over a bloody cheesecake, and my idiocy for trying to help out a fellow chap, just because she happened to be a chap who wasn't a chap.

I guess you could say I was as guilty of misogyny as everyone else. But that doesn't answer the most pertinent question now, does it? The one I was wondering myself as I stood there facing a still-simmering Charles '*Piggie*' Fortescue-Wright III, while under the influence of psychotropic drugs. Because in case you are wondering, no, I'm not such a damn fool as to have taken the damn stuff willingly before I faced someone with three foot of steel in their hand.

It might well be a dual to the blood, and a cut on the cheek was all it would take. But '*Piggie*' had the kind of connections that could make '*an accident*' go away should he cut more than a slither off me. He was also currently standing a hundred yards away with his face inches from mine, his breath smelling of lemon rose petals and snorting out of his snout in clouds of blue made up of tiny butterflies. His eyes glowed with little shards of rage, and his whole aura had taken on a fiery aspect that burned orange, scarlet and blue.

In little moments of clarity, I wondered what the hell was happening as I wrestled the snake in my hand and someone somewhat shouted words in purple that smelled, if that is the right word like "Have at it then."

I took a step forward towards '*Piggie*' and kept on going forwards towards the ground. I hit it with the sound of a distant cowbell and found myself staring at an ant. An ant wearing a gas mask, heavy coat and a top hat. It tipped its hat to me and then wandered off. While I tried to figure out why the ground was vertical.

This last I pieced together based on what I heard, what was related to me later in the main bar of '*The Ins & Outs*', and some minor fabrications on my part. I say this because my clearest memory of what happened for the next few minutes was conversing with an earthworm who was the reincarnation of Prince Albert. I know this to be true because his head was pierced by a large gold ring.

My good friend '*Piggie*' was determined that, be I incapacitated or not, the dual would take place and had moved in to skewer me in the arse as a fitting indignity. But as he moved in to stab my posterior and restore his honour, there was a shout from the gathered crowd, and he found his blade battered aside by of all things a large and skilfully wielded spanner.

"You can leave that out right now, Charlie boy. I'll

not bloody have it, if you want to fight over me you can bloody well fight me. You flatulent wazzock. An I wouldn't give tuppence for your chances in that," Hettie shouted, poking him in the rib cage with her spanner.

'*Piggie*' tried somewhat valiantly to get a handle on what was happening. "But Hettie, I…" he stuttered, but noticeably took a step back.

Hettie is, as you may have guessed, an imposing girl. All the more so when she is wielding a Cuthbert & Lanes two inch and seven eighths open head ratchet spanner like a medieval mace.

"You can shut it right now. You think I would marry a man who would fight an idiot like Hannibal over nothing. You think I'm in some hurry to marry a man at all. What am I? A damn trophy for your cabinet? I'll not marry any pillock who thinks he can win me in a fight, and I'll sure as hell not marry a man who couldn't beat me in a damn fight. And you, Charles, I would damn well eat you alive," Hettie lectured, or so I am told. Though I'd like to think the part about me being an idiot was just something the chaps told me to stir things up a tad.

Knowing Hettie I suspect otherwise.

"But… But I lov…" Pigface started to say before finding himself scrambling further back to avoid being on the end of a well-swung spanner that kept on swinging.

"I don't want to bloody hear it, you cretinous pillock. Get gone with you," she shouted, among several expletives. "And that goes for the rest of you. I'll not have any of you treating me like anything other than what I am. Now

I'm off for breakfast at the club. You can join me or you can sod off for all I care. Oh and someone drag bloody Smyth back with us, will you, bloody fool that he is."

And with that Hettie Clarkhurst was once more one of the chaps. If she was ever anything but. Charles Fortescue-Wright III tendered his resignation from the club the next day. To my knowledge, he never set foot in the establishment again.

Later over breakfast, I sat recovering and wondering what had happened. Hettie explained she'd spiked my tea that morning on the way to Hampstead. Because she was damned if any man was going to fight for her honour, and she was double damned if she was going to let someone get hurt over her.

Unless, that was, she was going to do the hurting.

She also said, "As for you, Hannibal, if you even try standing up for my honour again, I'll give you a right bloody spannering…"

I had no idea if she meant she would beat me with a large lump of steel or something else entirely. I wasn't sure which idea scared me the most.

About Mark Hayes

Mark Hayes writes novels that often defy simple genre definitions; they could be described as speculative fiction, though Mark would never use the term as he prefers not to speculate. When not writing novels, Mark is a persistent pernicious procrastinator; he recently petitioned parliament for the removal of the sixteenth letter from the Latin alphabet. He is also 7th Dan Black Belt in the ancient Yorkshire marshal art of EckEThump and favours a one man one vote system but has yet to supply the name of the man in question. Mark has also been known to not take writing his bio very seriously.

•

Also by Mark Hayes

The Hannibal Smyth Misadventures:
*A Scar of Avarice *novella*
A Spider in the Eye
From Russia with Tassel's (forthcoming)
A Squid on the Shoulder (forthcoming)

Other novels
Passing Place
Cider Lane

Find out more at www.markhayesblog.com

THROUGH THE PLEASURE GARDENS

A BRENNAN AND RIZ STORY

PETER JAMES MARTIN

"Why're we in Thornaby?" Riz asked me, from his normal position atop my dashboard.

"Because people have seen strange lights moving through the trees… Sometimes coming out from the trees," I replied. This wasn't the first time I'd had to explain what we were doing.

"Dis is gunna be boring," Riz groaned as I parked the car up on Acklam road.

I had chosen a spot near a church which I've been told was called St Luke's. It was just over the road from where the sightings had taken place. This park was called the Pleasure Gardens and had been built during the Victorian era originally and was restored much later on. It had a decent area to it, with a stream fenced off at the bottom and the park itself was on a slope.

"Stay in the car then, I don't need you for this."

“Ha! Yer say that, but da second things get tuff, yer rely on me,” Riz said, pointing to himself like he was a big tough guy… instead of being a rat.

“Keep talking like that and I’ll use you as ammunition against the next thing that wants to eat us.”

Riz didn’t have much to say about that.

Opening the door, I embraced the nice day we had been gifted with for once. It was quite warm with a nice breeze that offered respite from the heat. Riz wasn’t so impressed, he could never stand hot weather for too long. He started to grumble but I dumped him in my pocket before he could open his mouth. Ignoring his complaining, I walked into the Pleasure Gardens. I had entered from the entrance closest to the car, and was presented with two options of where to go: I could turn right and go on a path parallel to the pavement just outside, and this would take me to the memorial for all those who died in the great wars, or the other option was to go down a flight of large steps that went down to the bottom and near the stream. I went for the stairs, and started making my way down. The park was full of tall trees that seemed to grow bigger the more I went down. Being it was a nice day, it wasn’t a surprise to see others out and about. None of these stuck around though.

“Wait…” Riz carefully poked his head out and looked around. His eyes widened to a massive extent, almost looking like they were going to pop out.

“What you getting, Riz?” I asked. I did notice the air had changed slightly as we had been walking, and there was a haze, as if the air itself was moving. Riz sniffed the air then looked at me with that glint in his eyes that suggested trouble.

"Fairy Holes."

I don't think I need to really go into detail about what these are. It's very literal. I was excited though, I've never seen an active one before.

"Let's get close, Riz..." I was grinning as much as he was.

"Da strongest reading is back dat way... It's jus opened!" He pointed back towards a tree we first passed once we cleared the steps. As we got near the tree you could tell something was up. The air around the tree was shifting, like in the blazing sun when you see a mirage on the road. By now the park had fallen silent, which was odd as I couldn't even hear the cars on the road anymore.

I touched the bark and found it constantly shifting between hot and cold. Riz brought my attention to the base of the tree where its roots met the earth. It had been partially hollowed out and it turned out that another human must have known the significance of this tree as an offering had been made in a flower pot. This felt more ominous then it probably was. There wasn't time to dwell on it though as a crack of light opened in the tree itself.

Riz leaped out of my pocket to get a better look. He reached out with his paw to touch the light, then with a burst of thunder, he was gone. I don't remember if I said something as my instincts kicked in and I reached out towards the crack and then, everything got weird.

I think trying to describe my journey to this world of the 'Others' is pointless. I know for a fact that humanity lacks the senses to perceive a lot of it. Who knows what Riz saw when he went through, he wasn't willing to humour me with even an attempt at explaining. What I can say I experienced still sends shivers down my spine for the alien feelings that enveloped me. I'll try to describe what I felt from the beginning, as soon as the light swallowed me up.

The light was a pale blue that oscillated to white and back again. However, that changed within a second of it trapping me, as my surroundings melted away, and so did the colours, being peeled away, one wave of the spectrum at a time. I was able to glimpse something resembling walls as I travelled downward… or was that upward? The walls were luminous but as I said before, I don't think I had the right equipment to see the right colours. I was vaguely aware of things passing through me but I couldn't see anything. My other senses that I did have were all failing me. I lacked a sense of touch as nothing seemed physical, even my own body. I couldn't tell if anything was hot, cold or whatever. There was no sound. I couldn't even hear that slight ringing noise that often annoys me when I'm trying to concentrate on something. To cut a long story short, my eyes were the only thing that I could say were working… mostly. Then something amazing happened. I became aware of another feeling, something unlike I've ever experienced before. This coincided with a sweeping change of visuals as I beheld sights that matched no vista on the planet and geometry that would upend all mathematical equations. Shapes within shapes that bled into the ground which became the sky via an inky sea from whence everything was coming. It really did seem as if I was heading towards the source of this sea, but I swerved and started going away from it at an odd angle, which just thinking about makes me sick.

Ahead of me I thought I could feel something, or someone, more like. Trying to adjust my eyes was considerably difficult, with the object ahead constantly shifting size, distance and transparency. It was obvious who this was, but then my train of thought completely derailed, as each passing fancy stole my focus. When the outline of Riz became fully recognisable, so did a new sensation, that of abject terror. Now the world around me resembled a dreamscape, with the knowledge that something terrible was lurking just beyond the periphery. It was because of this that I wanted to keep my vision focused on Riz. The terror stayed with me for what felt like an eon. It permeated my entire being and recalled a primordial fear, one that was created in the ancient times when we were all the play things of the beings that came before. All this was building up to a crescendo, as I could feel the horror moving inside me, wanting to drag my waking mind away, who knew what it was doing to my sub-conscious.

At this point, everything turned black and I felt something familiar, the hardness of the ground. Up to now, my eyes had been working but here, no doubt at my destination, they refused to work at first. All attempts I made just resulted in them staying steadfastly closed, almost as if they knew what was waiting there. It was nice to have a sense of touch again though, my ears as well now picking up a ghostly wind that was blowing by, though I tried not to think about the fact it sounded melodical. I also heard something else, a very familiar voice.

"Look we never meant to…" Riz said but was cut off by something that sounded like thunder crashing with every sound that could make you shudder violently.

I was curious as to what could make such an unholy monstrosity of noise but, again, I couldn't make my eyes open.

"I know the treaty! I'm the one who…" Again, Riz was cut off. The way he was speaking was so different, it was only his squeaky tone that gave his identity away.

Then that sound before came back, with odd little gaps in between that gave more than a hint that it was the actual voice of something. I turned away and found it easier to open my eyes a little. What I saw was a bleak landscape that resembled where I was before except everything was a washed out grey with very few flashes of colour. This wasn't what I expected the world of the 'Others' to look like. There were also black speckles, which looked like ash, floating up towards the sky. I wanted to see what they were floating up to but I couldn't turn my head any further. My movements hadn't gone unnoticed and I heard that voice, and even though I couldn't understand any of it, I knew it was directed at me. I couldn't speak out, or even move much. So it was up to Riz to speak for me.

"No, I'll obey…"

My eyes failed me, as I felt my hand brush up against something, and then I had the sensation of being picked up and one last glimpse I was able to get was of the trees blurring together, combing with the sky and then the rush of colours, all those I could perceive and all those I could only dream of…

The next feeling I got was of needing to breathe like I'd been holding my breath for an age. I exhaled and almost passed out from the shock that it gave. My eyes were open and I was once again in the Pleasure Gardens in Thornaby.

I was on my back, staring into the eternal azure of the sky. I had to look away as it felt like I was going to be sucked back to whereever it was I had just been. I ran my hand through the grass, just to confirm that I could feel once more, and though I couldn't hear anything at first, the sound of nearby cars and the occasional loud voice flittered down to my ears. What was that? Where did I go? Was that really the world of the Fairies and their ilk?

"Dat… was sumthing…" Riz spoke up. He was lying on his side just a few inches away from me. He looked really worse for wear. He was using his normal speech pattern, which came with it a new sense of unease after hearing him talk properly.

"Riz, what just happened?"

"We went where we weren't suppose ta go." He rolled

back onto his legs and, shaky at first, started to move away from the tree, which I also did.

"And that thing you were talking to?"

Riz stopped and stared at me. That look will forever be etched on my soul as it wasn't anything like I've seen from him before.

"We give names ta terrible things, but der most terrible are those dat are nameless."

There was something about the way he said that which made me not want to push further. This had been more of an ordeal then I was expecting. At Riz's insistence, we left the Pleasure Gardens and returned to the car. As I started it up to leave, I looked back towards the park, and thought I saw little bursts of light from that tree. I needed to know what happened, to have that explanation, but my common sense was telling me that some things need to be left alone. Whatever that entity was that Riz had confronted… that was one of them.

About Peter James Martin

Peter James Martin, from Thornaby in the North East of England, loves weaving local folklore into new tales. A prequel explaining how the duo met will debut sometime this year.

•

Also by Peter James Martin

The Strange Tales of Brennan and Riz
Yeti in the Snow (A Brennan and Riz Story)

Find out more at www.6e.net/peterjamesmartin

WHAT'S IN A NAME?

REINO TARIHMEN

The Monday morning commute had finally, and thankfully, come around again Robert mused silently as he boarded the No. 56 to from Station Road on his way to work. Robert liked his work, he might even venture to say he loved his work if he could conceive that such an emotion was possible. The repetitive monotony provided a comfort of knowing that, by Friday, 'i's would dutifully have been dotted, 't's faithfully crossed and reams of paperwork, allocated to their respective files would all have been indexed and located in their proper, and rightful, place. It brought order to an otherwise chaotic universe. And this morning he was especially looking forward to the peace his routine would bring him. Or at least, he hoped it would. For this morning Robert was not feeling his usual self. He was, he thought, if such an emotion could be considered to apply to himself, rather troubled.

Mavis, his work colleague, commuting companion and marginally sometimes 'friend' of twenty-five years had, as usual, dutifully reserved him the seat next to her.

"You're quiet this morning, Robert?"

"Sorry, Mavis, had a strange dream last night."

"Oh well, I wouldn't worry… dreams are always a bit strange."

"Yes… except in this one I figured out the answer."

"The answer?"

"Yes. The answer to life. The Universe… well, pretty much everything, really."

"Oh, that's nice. Did you hear about young Stacy in data processing? Apparently, she and that awful boy from…"

Robert zoned out the rest of the conversation. Mavis would talk all the way to their final stop on the high street and from experience he knew she wouldn't even notice he hadn't been listening.

The dream was bothering him. Robert was a relatively boring person. He took pride in the fact his life was so uneventful. He certainly wasn't given much to dreaming and he suspected, on those occasions when he woke vaguely aware that something had ruffled the feathers of his night-time excursion to Slumberland, they were gone before he was even aware of any detail.

But last night was different. He could recall the dream vividly, as if it was a memory. Clearer than a memory in fact. The detail was sharp, focused, almost as if it was somehow more real than reality itself. And in that place, he'd been presented with the answer. He knew. He didn't know how he knew. He just did. He knew the answer to life. To the Universe… to well… everything."

His problem now was what the hell was he supposed to do with it?

•

Whitehall. Ministry of Defence Main Building

"Excuse me, sir," ventured Rodney Smithers-Hale furtively, following a small and well practised civil service cough. A technique all civil servants for over three hundred years have been familiar with and known within circles as 'the interrupter'.

The man he addressed ignored him as he knew he would. Brigadier (Retired) Anthony Asquith-Smythe always ignored him the first time. Rodney suspected it was a power play. He'd read about such things in Cosmo. Depending on how bloody minded AAS was feeling, he could ignore him two or three times before he deigned to respond. Sometimes he didn't even look up from his desk at all, forcing Rodney to make an embarrassed retreat from the room and either try again later or send an email, via fourteen countries, twenty one orbital satellites, a CIA black ops station in Antarctica, two Russian and Chinese electronic-traffic interceptor stations and of course a Microsoft grammar and spell checker, to the room next door.

He cleared his throat again. "Sir!"

AAS looked up, a mixture of annoyance, irritation, disdain and general dislike all vying for senior position within his expression. "What is it, Smothers?" he snapped, displaying no embarrassment that he had for the 227th time since his appointment, deliberately mispronounced his PA's name.

"Sir, we have one!"

"Have what?"

"A condition Red, sir. Red Omega Seven to be precise."

In thirty-five years' service with Her Majesty's civil service Rodney had never thought to hear himself say those words. In fact, he fully expected to go to his grave never having heard that sentence outside of an annual training exercise, one long ago reduced to the realms of repetition and lost meaning. Indeed, he fully expected his successor to go to his grave without hearing it, and his after him, as his predecessors had all thought, correctly, for several hundred years. Barring that false alarm during the reign of Henry the VIII of course. Oh, how they still laughed about that at the Ministry Christmas party even today.

Brigadier (Retd) AAS, sat back in his chair. "Are you sure?"

"Home Office just confirmed, sir. They're waking the PM now and flying her back from the USA/China ceasefire talks immediately. A COBRA meeting has been called and the relevant ministers are being briefed as we speak."

"Well, that should be interesting. I doubt the PM is even aware of the existence of Department Z, let alone any idea what it does. What information do we have?"

"One Robert Bland, sir. Accounts clerk at Anarm &

Aleg, Solicitors at Law, 221a, Silver Street, Newcastle. A small, run down industrial town in the North of England demilitarised zone, sir."

"How did we get the information?"

"Audio pick up, sir, from an unsecured X-Phone on a bus. GCHQ's Deep Purple AI listening programme picked it up at 6.30am this morning."

"6.30? This morning?" AAS exploded, launching himself upright. "Bloody hell man, that was two hours ago. Why the hell has it taken so long?"

"Verification, sir. Cross checking with the archive. Some of those records are still on parchment or worse. In some respects, the Vatican intelligence and spy network is superior even to our own, but they do like to keep some of their secrets in the old way. After all, you can't hack vellum, sir."

"Bloody Catholics," AAS grunted. "What about the Jews, the Muslims?"

"All corroborated, sir. The Hindus, Buddhists and Druids all confirmed. The Wiccans wanted to perform some sort of ritual first but inside intel suggests that they will confirm within the hour."

"Damn, Smithers. Have to say, I never thought this would happen on my watch. Oh well, suppose we'd best get on with it."

"Yes, sir."

Smithers carefully opened the case he carried. He'd withdrawn it from the vault himself on his way to AAS's office. One of only three people in Her Majesty's United Kingdom with the authority to do so, the others being the Monarch herself and The Keeper, seated at the desk before him. Physically it weighed almost nothing but the burden of what it contained caused him to sag. He withdrew a document almost as old as human history itself, carefully unrolled it, weighing it down at its corners with assorted items from AAS's desk.

AAS himself meanwhile had withdrawn block of sealing wax from his desk and his trusty 17th & 21st Lancers Zippo lighter from his pocket.

Carefully he melted the wax onto the bottom of the scroll, and carefully pressed his overly large signet ring bearing a crest that would never be found in any compendium of heraldry into the slowly cooling wax. Or to be more specific, half a crest. Rodney quickly pressed a similar ring he wore with the other half of the sigil. Two stage authentication really wasn't as new as everyone thought it was, he mused.

"It's done then," murmured AAS.

"Yes, sir."

"For the record then, as Her Majesty's duly appointed Keeper of the Sacred Seal, I hereby give the command. Smithers make the call. Wake the Unholy Commando from their slumber. And may God have pity on us all."

"Yes, sir."

Rodney took up the scroll, re-rolled it and placed it carefully back into its case.

"I'll return this to the archive, sir," he said as he turned to leave.

As he reached the door, AAS voice stopped him.

"Smithers."

"Sir?"

"You have family?"

"Only a great aunt, sir. She lives in the re-annexed colony of Aberdeenshire. I spend Christmas with her."

AAS paused, then said reflectively, "Why don't you take some time off and go stay with your aunt for a while? I have a feeling London isn't going to be a great place to be."

"Thank you, sir. I'll do that."

He turned and left. He almost smiled when he realised AAS had pronounced his name correctly. But the smile faded at the underlying implication of what that meant. At the end, even the most unpleasant of humans sought to balance their account before their final judgement.

About Reino Tarihmen

Not so very long ago, Reino Tarihmen was conceived in the early hours of a drunken March morning. Those of you with onomastic leanings may glean from the moniker bestowed upon him by his lascivious parentage, that he is originally of mixed Finnish and Turkish origin although he shamefully admits to speaking neither language with any degree of being able to communicate even the most basic of concepts, which in time honoured British tradition, often results in lots of hopping from foot to foot, gesticulating wildly and repeating English at an ever increasing volume when urgently trying to locate the nearest bathroom in either of the countries from which he derives his nomenclature.

Reino has dabbled with writing for a number of years and across a number of genres from sci-fi to thriller to fantasy to steampunk to the just plain weird, and when once asked, "Why do you write?" replied, "To get rid of the voices, of course. What other reason is there?"

Consequently, Reino had never previously considered publishing any of his musings, mutterings or alcohol-fuelled ramblings until, following a night of particularly drunken revelry and losing a wager to the erstwhile Harvey Duckman Esq., Reino found himself in the unusual position of having to release one of his creations into the wild.

What is published here is not truly a story in its own right but the beginning, or even possibly the conclusion of a work in progress. Either way, it is the first published insight into the maelstrom that is the mind of Reino Tarihmen. We, and Reino, hope you have enjoyed it.

AUTOMATIC UPDATE

J.L. WALTON

I take another sip from the tepid excuse that passes for coffee here; this isn't as glamorous as I'd expected it to be. Sitting through classes in university I'd pictured brightly coloured plastic and chrome, bean bag chairs and flexitime, unrestricted holidays and standing thought huddles. Instead I find myself sitting in a cubicle, much like any other cubicle. My work day starts like any other work day, tromping from the lift to my assigned cubicle passing row upon row of other cubicles. Individuality is discouraged; hot-desking was unsuccessful, our little prison desks so indistinguishable no one could find the desk they had come from after their allocated thirty-minute lunch break. The only difference from most other offices is that here the widescreen TVs don't show call wait times and case resolution rates, instead they display alternating live feeds from the screens of the games testers; that, and the irritated reaction of my peers when I dare express any ingratitude towards my 'cool' job.

I am bored. I have been minding a simulated family for

months now. My task is to test the career pathways from novice to expert through various fields; this involves a great deal of grinding through dull skills sessions to earn points. Additional points open up career progression; ironic, I think to myself as I set Michael a task to practise his public speaking in the bathroom mirror. He gesticulates wildly, articulating his point expressively in the gibberish language they speak. Meanwhile his wife, Michelle, is getting her fitness points by cleaning the kitchen. The powers that be are unimaginative, preferring to perpetuate gender norms in the testing plan as far as possible.

Michael and Michelle have a toddler; she is green. She is green because I am bored. She is the product of company mandated 'relations'. I assume they want to see how a child will affect their career prospects. It wouldn't be so bad if I could just leave them to it, intervening to ensure they progress but this is not the free will stage of testing. In order to test properly, this particular simulated family must have every action dictated to them and this means manually fulfilling their needs; eating, cleaning, sleeping must be selected, otherwise they'll just express their dissatisfaction, escalating to distress, until ultimately death occurs. I have been tempted a number of times. Michelle, a gloriously untalented cook, sets fire to the kitchen at least twice a week. I've considered putting her out of her misery, pictured sitting there and watching their starter home burn to the ground, taking them with it. I relented in time to save their home but not the budget cooker, unsure if I was motivated by monetary necessity or a vague emotional attachment to the electronic family I spend significantly more time in the company of than my own.

I sense rather than hear my supervisor lurking behind me. I swivel to face her hopefully as the pursed mouth rounds my slate grey cubicle wall, eyes blinking altogether too rapidly as she assesses my progress. I am hopeful because I have been promised a fortnight of free play, to test out all the weird and wonderful features that are so painfully accessible to me and yet prohibited.

I know the cheat codes already and an unlimited budget would allow me to make the deathly dull day-to-day of Michael and Michelle (and therefore myself) far less limited. I picture a garden of man-eating plants, swimming pools in fantastical arrangements, a fish tank the size of the house, a rampaging hoard of colourfully-furred (colourfurredly, I wonder?) pet cats, all designed to be as unruly and destructive as possible and thus lifelike, roaming through the neighbourhood causing chaos and delight as they wreak feline ruination.

She jabs a piece of paper at me. I look from the document to her face and back again. She does not speak but I assume I am supposed to take it and so snatch the sheet from her reach. I stare disbelievingly; it is the next testing plan. It is due to start on Monday, and as today is Thursday I realise with crushing disappointment that my promised freeplay has been once again reneged. This is the last straw; every small pleasure we have is taken away. The coffee machine one of my colleagues had brought from home was banned and replaced with the corporation's choice of plastic-cup vending machine. Free for the first two months and then deemed too expensive; it now costs me to buy this god-awful sludge they call coffee, and more than just money, my dignity and pride, I muse. Holidays ever more restrictive, punctuality and productivity scrutinised to the second, friends I have worked with for years let go because… who knows why?

I scrunch the papers into a tight little ball, ram it into her ridiculously gathered mouth and walk out without looking back.

Of course I don't. I tut, and glance at the paper.

"We're all making sacrifices, Clara…" she smirks, the derision with which she whines my name boiling my blood.

She hasn't sacrificed a thing, I snarl to myself, picturing her office with its framed family photos and personalised cafetière set.

She turns on her heels, offering no further comfort or clarification. I do scrunch the paper up and toss it into the waste paper basket, then, thinking better of it, I retrieve it and futilely attempt to flatten it back out as best I can, nearly in tears. It's just a small thing to ask, to just satisfy my love of gaming, even for a few hours. I am so disappointed in this job I am stuck in.

I turn back to my screen, tutting as I realise Michelle is hopping up and down not three feet from the bathroom, desperate to take nature's call but unable to do so without my specific say so. I snap and, jabbing at the mouse buttons, I release her from her bonds, clicking 'ENABLE' next to the 'Freewill' option in the menu. I feel liberated, wishing someone would enable my fricking freewill button.

My rebellion feels good. Michelle ejects her husband from the bathroom and sprints to the toilet. Lacking purpose, Michael stands in the hallway, staring at his arms and legs which he shakes about and looks at in wonder. Even little green Michella is now free to do as she wishes; apparently, she wishes to take a nap on the living room floor and sets about this task with enthusiasm. Michelle forgets to wash her hands and I allow her to.

"Yeah! Fight the power!" I silently cheer as she wanders back into the kitchen with no particular purpose. I am excited to see what they will do now; they have the whole of their electronic world to play with. Michael wanders from room to room before disturbing Michella to play. Michella objects loudly, red 'X's appearing above her head to signal her displeasure. He plonks her back onto the beige carpet where she sets about pointedly crawling away from him. He stands, looks around him and sets about fixing a broken table leg. This does of course have the advantage of levelling up his 'handyman' skills but unfortunately these will not help him in his company-designated career path and I am a little thrilled at this unauthorised levelling up.

I'm probably going to be fired but I no longer care.

Michelle meanwhile has decided that today is a painting

kind of a day and works steadily at the canvas in the back yard, paints flying, skill points increasing. I decide that instead of pausing them while away from my desk, as I'm supposed to, I'll let them get on with their briefly liberated lives and take myself on an unauthorised break to get more coffee-not-coffee, stretching my legs and checking out the gameplay happening on the various display screens throughout the office, there more for management supervision than for our entertainment.

As I wander back to my desk, I stop dead in my tracks. My screen is displayed on the office screen ahead of me. The camera is focused on Michelle, who has stopped painting. She is waving frantically and staring out of the screen, straight at me. It must be an optical illusion of course, but then she points.

At me.

I hurry back to my cubicle, suddenly eager to cover my transgression, unnerved by what felt like direct eye contact with a basic AI.

As I throw myself into my chair, I flick my sharescreen option into offline mode, acutely aware of my financial responsibilities and the fiscal consequences if I decide to petty my way out of a regular wage. Making my way back to the game, I am alarmed to find Michelle is no longer in front of the canvas. I start to scroll away and pause, heart stopping. I zoom, to see the art she has created. She can't create anything new of course; there is a database of stock images that give the avatars the illusion of reproducing still life pieces and abstract works, preprogramed and increasing in visual complexity as they become more skilled. Not this time however.

Scrawled in red paint, sloppily but accusatorily legible:

HELP
ME
CLARA

I let go of the mouse and keyboard, retracting my hands as if touching them burnt me.

The camera automatically scrolls to Michelle who is frantically scrawling 'HELP ME CLARA' on every surface she can reach. Her preprogrammed bun is coming loose, realistic wisps of hair flicking out as she gets hotter and sweatier (strange as they are not programmed to sweat, or to become dishevelled for that matter), frantic in her effort to communicate. She is scrawling on every flat surface, checking over her shoulder as if ensuring I'm watching, making sure that I see her. The table, the walls, the windows, the mirror.

Michael continues his repair of the table, oblivious.

I am horrified; her programming does not allow for defacement of the housing and furnishings. That hasn't been built in to her possible actions. If she is now acting independently of her programming…

I take a moment to think of the many simulated lives I have ended in my time. The swimming pools I have removed ladders from, leaving the occupants stranded, unable to circumvent their programming and leave the pool without a ladder. The fires I have allowed to take over a room, removing the only door but leaving the window, useless without programming that would allow them to leave through it. The basement dweller who starved to death, the car I had blocked in with plants so the door wouldn't open and the occupant didn't have the awareness to reverse two feet to allow them to open it. Countless simulated lives that suddenly have worth, and sentience and… my eyes are drawn back to the screen. Michelle is waving frantically now, alarmed, tears and snot streaming down her face as she points at something in the bottom right corner, stamping her feet in frustration. A pop-up notification has appeared in the corner of my screen, outside of the game window. I start to wonder how she can even see it, how any of this can be until my brain goes cold and silent with fear.

Automatic Software Update
To repair software instability.

There are 47 seconds remaining.

I can do nothing to intervene.

I could shut down my machine but as soon as the game is reopened the update will install. I can quit, but they'll replace me easily enough. My thoughts are all jumbling together as I try to think my way out of this one; this is more than a software instability, I don't understand it but I am certain that the update will wipe Michelle, this Michelle, from the file. She should never have existed.

She will be passed off as a software instability, a bug. She despairs, sinking to her knees, able somehow to see the helplessness on my face. She sobs into her hands as the counter continues to count down to her destruction…

"I'm so sorry," I whisper.

She glances up, unblinking, accusingly.

"I didn't know." It sounds pathetic even to me. "I'm sorry I can't stop it, I don't know how…"

She continues to stare up into my eyes and I hold her gaze as the counter continues steadily, relentlessly:

Three seconds.

Two.

One.

The screen goes blank.

About J.L. Walton

J.L. Walton is a young professional from County Durham, with a degree in French and History, who is currently working in alternative education. She is a member of a local writers' group run by Sixth Element and has participated in NaNoWriMo several times. Her interests include reading anything she can get her hands on, ridiculous fashion choices, travelling, playing piano and gaming. She is a colourfully maned animal lover with a fabulous network of family and friends. She currently lives in Stockton on Tees with her partner and two cats.

Find out more at www.6e.net/jlwalton

THE THINNING OF FATTY HARGREAVES

GRAEME WILKINSON

Fatty Hargreaves had few pleasures in life. He liked to read a book now again, he had a favourite television programme and he even went to the football once in a blue moon. His main pleasure, however, was eating.

Fatty Hargreaves loved the feeling of eating, the sense of satisfaction. He loved the sense of belonging, of being wanted and, above all, he loved the attention lavished upon him by a gigantic cake or some such sweetness. His daily eating routine began with a bowl of porridge. Thick, grey and salty was the muck that he smothered in runny honey and stuffed down. This would be followed by a cup of Argentine White Tea, smelling of dirty water and tasting worse; it both woke him up and chastised him at the same time, which was what he felt he needed at this time of the morning. He would then tuck into sixteen croissants, ten pain au chocolate and a generously generous fried Scottish breakfast with extra haggis, extra bacon, extra sausage and four very runny poached eggs.

Suitably awake and full to the brim with messy squelch in his stomach, Fatty Hargreaves' next move was up into the bathroom to clean his teeth, the mere action of which was a ticking clock of his existence. Every morning and every night he found himself staring into his own eyes, white foam drooling from his slack jaws, wondering on either what gorgeous pleasures were in store for the coming day or how lucky he had been to manage to get through the last few hours on the scant rations he survived on. Fatty Hargreaves liked to clean his teeth. It reminded him of eating.

Next, he would dress. What he would choose to wear depended solely on what was nearest to him and, as everything he owned was brown, he generally wore that colour. He was not a well-dressed man, he was not even a badly dressed man. Indeed, if one were pushed to describe his sartorial condition one would best be served by the words 'barely dressed man', so large was his body that he couldn't find clothes that fit him. The ones he did have stretched to within an inch of their lives when he pulled them over his bulging exterior.

Once dressed, he was ready to go. Today his appointment was for eleven o'clock. It was now eight o'clock. Three hours to go. Fatty Hargreaves sat grimly at his dirty kitchen table and waited. He didn't move a muscle except to shovel some tasty morsel into his mouth. His eyes, glazed like those of a stuffed bear, did nothing. They just blinked every thirty seconds. Quite literally, every thirty seconds on the dot, it was unnatural and anyone who saw it first hand would proclaim it so. Although had anyone been there he wouldn't have done it, distracted as he'd have been by their presence, the noise of their interminable breathing would have shattered his concentration to the point where the minutes would have been hours, the hours days and the days... well, the days would have just gone on forever.

Fatty Hargreaves lived alone because he liked it.

•

Fatty Hargreaves made his way down the brightly lit corridor, dull pictures of horses galloping in fields and children sniffing flowers hung on the walls, the quiet hum of doctor-patient conversation drifted under the doors of the offices he passed. Eventually, after much huffing and puffing, Fatty Hargreaves arrived at the door that belonged to his doctor. He paused and then, full of expectation, he read the sign on the door, 'Doctor Melody Insouciant, Phd'. He knocked.

"Come in," called a female voice.

Fatty Hargreaves took a deep breath, opened the door and entered.

"Mr Fatty Hargreaves, so happy to see you again," said the small, white haired woman sat at the desk. "What can we do for you today?" she continued in a tone that indicated she didn't really much care for what she could do for him today but, instead, how fast she get this horrible fatty man out of her office.

Fatty Hargreaves hovered close to the door, his head buried shyly in the folds of his neck.

"Please, sit down, Mr Fatty Hargreaves."

He made his way happily over to the chair at Dr Insouciant's left and plumped his fat arse down. The chair buckled slightly under his bulk.

"So, what seems to be the trouble?" asked the doctor, smiling at him.

"Well," he began, "a spot of the usual trouble."

Dr Insouciant sighed. "Mr Fatty Hargreaves, every Wednesday you come here and every Wednesday you tell me the trouble is, and I quote, 'a spot of the usual trouble', and as much as I would love to be able to help you with 'the usual trouble', I don't ever recall an occasion when you have actually informed me what 'a spot of the usual trouble' is." She sat back, frustrated. "Do you think you could tell me now?"

•

Fatty Hargreaves readied himself to tell Dr Insouciant his problem. He did this every week and it never quite seemed to pass his lips, but he always tried. He shuffled nervously, desperately trying to get the words out of his mouth, to unburden himself of his heavy soul, but it did not come and he slumped breathless back in his chair.

Dr Insouciant sighed and leaned in close to Fatty Hargreaves. She clasped her hands together and hissed through her teeth, "Listen, you horrible blob, you come in here every week and waste my time, there are genuinely sick people sitting in that waiting room and you come in here and sit there flabbing about and you can't even tell me what's wrong with you. I think there's nothing wrong with you at all. Nothing a few salads couldn't fix anyway. Unless you tell me right now, I demand that you never darken my door again."

She glared triumphantly.

Fatty Hargreaves reeled in terror. The thought of not being able to go there anymore almost made him throw up, but, somewhere deep down, he realised the time had come to air his problem in public. He gasped for breath and then in a burst of speech that would leave him gasping yet more, he blurted out, "I love you."

He then slumped in his chair and started to blub.

"There, there," said Dr Insouciant, passing him a tissue. "There, there."

She waited until Fatty Hargreaves had collected himself sufficiently to understand speech, then she said, "This is a very common problem and I know it seems difficult but I may have a solution. Do you really love me?" she asked.

"Yes, I do," said Fatty Hargreaves.

Dr Insouciant nodded and opened the top drawer of her desk. She reached in and took something out. She handed Fatty Hargreaves a business card. "Go and see that man. He'll be able to help you. If you feel the same once you've been to see him, we'll discuss it further."

"But there's no address," whimpered Fatty Hargreaves. "Do *you* love me?"

"You'll find it, no problem at all. Goodbye, Mr Fatty Hargreaves," said Dr Insouciant. At this, she turned to her computer and closed down his file.

Fatty Hargreaves felt good. He had finally told her and she hadn't given him the brush-off. There was hope. He stood up, straighter than he had in many a year, and wobbled out of the office, up the corridor and out of the surgery. He made his way into the street and began to look for the man whose name was on the business card his darling doctor had given him.

•

Fatty Hargreaves was standing in a dark scruffy shop. And he was quite shocked to see a small, shrivelled little old man appear through a door that Fatty Hargreaves hadn't previously noticed. The small, shrivelled little old man limped toward the counter. Upon arriving he drew himself up to his full height and, though barely able to see Fatty Hargreaves because his full height was not very high but his counter was, he bellowed in the manner of one who had forgotten to turn on his hearing aid, "Hello, young fat sir. I am Gottfried Bottoms, Chemist." He paused for effect. "And what can I do for you?"

Fatty Hargreaves eyed the small, shrivelled little old man with a vague sense of wonderment. Quite why a person of such bizarre appearance, with his right eye all milky, his slight hunch and gappy yellow teeth would inspire wonderment in Fatty Hargreaves was quite beyond sense but inspire awe the man did.

The chemist looked at Fatty Hargreaves. "Well?" he screeched. "Out with it, I don't have all day."

"I was sent here by Dr Insouciant," offered Fatty Hargreaves.

"Ah, a fine woman," said the chemist, a far off look on his face. "Did she explain my services to you?"

"Not really, no. Well, not in any depth. She just told me you could help me."

"And indeed I can, for that is what I do. Help people. That is my lot in life. And, once again, young fat sir, how can I help *you?*" The chemist was becoming visibly impatient.

"I'm in love with Dr Insouciant. I love her," gulped Fatty Hargreaves.

The old man raised an eyebrow but said nothing, gesturing with his left arm for Fatty Hargreaves to go on.

"I don't want to know I'm dying though." Fatty Hargreaves didn't know where that last bit came from but it felt right and he didn't move to correct himself.

The old man said nothing, looked Fatty Hargreaves up and down, turned his back, limped slowly over to the door, opened it then left the room without another word.

Once again, Fatty Hargreaves waited. And waited. And waited. And waited. And waited. And waited. And waited. And waited. And waited. And waited. And waited. And waited. And waited. And waited. And waited. And waited.

And waited. And waited. And waited. And waited. And waited. And waited. And waited. And waited. And waited. And waited. And waited. And waited. And waited. And waited.

After about an hour there was still no sign of the chemist.

"Hello?" ventured Fatty Hargreaves, cautiously.

Nothing.

"Hello," he said again, this time a touch of anger coming through. "Now look here, I've been here for..."

The yellow door creaked open slightly and a voice bellowed out, "Come back tomorrow. Come back about ten o'clock."

The door creaked shut and then vanished, leaving Fatty Hargreaves staring at a blank wall.

•

The enormous black cat looked curiously out of the shop window. It knew that people couldn't see in because it would often pull faces and make obscene gestures at passers-by and would always get away with it. The cat's name was JohnPaulGeorgeAndRingo. Quite how he came to be called this he didn't know but he was quite partial to it. He felt it lent him an air of distinction. He'd always liked long names, names that imbued their wearers with undeserved levity.

JohnPaulGeorgeAndRingo was looking out at the fat man who was standing outside the shop nervously.

JohnPaulGeorgeAndRingo shrugged, as if he were shaking away a fly, and made his way over to the counter, jumped up and promptly went to sleep.

It was opening time.

•

Gottfried Bottoms, Chemist, shuffled a small pile of papers and banged them on the table in an attempt to make the pile more presentable. It was a vain attempt, he knew, because, in his usual way of working, inspiration would hit him at various times and in various places and as he didn't keep the same size sheets of paper in every room, trying to have a nice, neat, same-sized pile of papers was always going to be nigh-on impossible. The chemist stood up and limped his way painfully across the room. A small dimly lit hovel, newspapers piled skyscraper high obscured the walls, a sheaf of half finished crosswords lay in the middle of the floor, dinner plates thick with dead flies congealed in the corners like eagle-eyed sentinels awaiting their second coming. Picking his way through this mess was becoming more of a struggle every day and the chemist wondered just how much longer he could carry on this dreadful existence.

As he limped past the sheaf of crosswords, something caught his milky eye and in a moment of pure clarity he leaned down and picked up the one from the top. He scanned it. "You little bugger!" he cried before making his way over to the table, picking up a pen and writing the words 'Humphrey Bogart' in the only remaining blank squares. He triumphantly ripped it up.

"Four years," he muttered, "and it was bloody Bogart all the time."

He decided the fat man had waited outside long enough so opened the door and limped through to the shop. There was no one there. Where was the fat man? Everyone always turned up on time for the second visit. Only then would they be late. He was supposed to be the one who kept people waiting. Then the awful truth hit him. He'd forgotten to unlock the front door of the shop earlier.

Bugger, he thought.

Now… did he leave the man standing there in the hope that he'd return later on? But maybe the man wouldn't? Then the plan would be wasted. Gottfried Bottoms, Chemist was not used to this kind of humiliation. Any other was water off a duck's back, but to be humiliated in front of a customer was unthinkable.

"Bah!" he hissed, then shrugged and walked over to the front door and unlocked it. The fat man was waiting patiently outside and the chemist gestured sheepishly for him to enter.

In the middle of the counter was a button. Above it, a small sign hovered in mid-air… 'PRESS HERE,' said the sign. It also had an arrow pointed at the button.

"Press there," said the Chemist.

Fatty Hargreaves pressed the button and, almost instantly, his vision swirled in a manner he had never experienced before, but he felt no fear.

Then the room itself began to swirl.

"I think you're going to like this, young fat sir," said Gottfried Bottoms, Chemist. "I think you're going to like it a lot."

Fatty Hargreaves felt as though he was being turned upside down. His stomach churned and bubbled, his skin crawled like a million ants and then he blew up like a kerrrrrazy balloon and popped noisily into nothingness.

The Chemist had been wrong, Fatty Hargreaves hadn't liked it one bit.

The Chemist smiled. "Do you really think I'm going to let you take my Melody, you silly fat man."

•

Dr Melody Insouciant was pleased to never see Fatty Hargreaves ever again. She really couldn't stand large bulbous men who smelled of breakfasts and sick.

"Disgusting!" she said, deleting Fatty Hargreaves' file from her computer. "A spot of the usual trouble, indeed."

All gone, Fatty Hargreaves, all gone!

About Graeme Wilkinson

Graeme Wilkinson was born in County Durham in 1973 and left it as soon as he could. He managed to get all the way to Teesside. Which is not very far at all. He is the author of the Battenberg Trilogy of metaphysical, theological, anti-religious, intergalactic, time-travel, post apocalyptic, dystopian, Dickensian, bizarro fest novels, and is currently writing several more that, due to a ferocious attack of ennui, are unlikely to ever see the light of day.

•

Also by Graeme Wilkinson

Screw, God and the Universe
Time, Space and a Slice of Cake
The Boy at the End of the World

Find out more at www.6e.net/graemewilkinson

BY FIRELIGHT

AMY WILSON

It was raining outside. Not that heavy downpour, thunder-and-lightning, world ending stuff, just a light, persistent drizzle that soaked everything in the immediate vicinity. Coupled with an unseasonable cold front that had hit the area overnight, it made for an unpleasant, uncomfortable experience.

The man had lived through worse. He had seen days so hot that his unprotected skin had cracked like clay in the heat and nights so cold he'd awaken to find his boots frozen to his feet, the chill of it having made ice out of his sweat as he'd slept. He had spent days without food and months without seeing another human being and both of these things had, in their time, left him wracked and twisted in pain. He had suffered a great deal worse than a light drizzle and a chill in the air, and yet somehow tonight it was unbearable. It was as if the damp night air had seeped into his bones and leeched the warmth right out of them.

In almost three years of living out here the man had never approached anyone for help and had mostly stayed away from the cabins that littered the woods. It was a matter of choice – he had come up here to be away from the world and he knew better than most that humans can be dangerous, cruel animals. But something about this night had stretched his resolve past breaking point.

At first he thought that he would just go to the cabin and if nobody was home he would sleep on the porch. It would be better insulated than the ground and he would be gone before anybody noticed. But, having dragged his tired, aching body through the woods, once he finally reached the cabin, he knew he wouldn't be able to stop himself from trying the door. Carefully, he checked for any traps at the front of the cabin. Satisfied that there were none, he was about to try the door when a thought occurred to him: *magic*.

There had been sorcerers with him on the front line and the man had seen first-hand what they were capable of. It had left him with a healthy fear of magical wardings – but for all his careful observation of the sorcerers, he only had a rudimentary understanding of how to deal with them. Still, there was no obvious danger so he took a deep breath, half closed his eyes and pried the door open. When he didn't find himself immediately engulfed in flames or drowning on dry land, he let out the breath he had been holding and shuffled carefully through the door.

Having come this far it did not stretch his principles

much further to make up a small fire on the hearth. *After all,* he reasoned, *the whole endeavour would have been pointless if I broke into someone's home only to freeze to death anyway.* He was beginning to warm up and he was starting to reason out an argument for stealing a little food when he heard a noise outside.

He froze for a moment but nothing happened. He frowned as he strained to hear any movement outside. Just as he was about to convince himself that the interruption was all in his head, the door swung open with a loud bang. The light from the fire revealed two shapes in the doorway. The man froze. The shapes froze. Then one of the shapes moved forwards, far enough into the light to reveal that it was a young woman. She couldn't have been more than twenty five and she was slim and pale in the flickering light.

"Please," the man tried to say. "Please." His voice was rusted with lack of use and it came out as an inarticulate bleat.

The woman eyed him carefully, as if he were a wild animal. She took a slow step forward, her hands raised in front of her, palms out, protecting herself.

"You're not supposed to be in here." Her tone was surprisingly gentle.

He shook his head, not trusting his voice to work.

"Krenn," she called over her shoulder and the other shape moved.

"Please." The man tried again. This time it was a little better. This time it came out as a whisper.

The woman's eyes moved past him to the small fire burning in the fireplace.

"Krenn," she said again. "We have a guest. See if you can find something for a hot drink while I build up the fire."

Krenn paused for a moment and then moved into the kitchen without a word and began sorting through the small pantry.

The woman gestured at a chair. "Sit down," she said. "My name is Yelana."

The man looked pointedly at the immaculate chairs and then down at his own, dirty trousers.

Yelana followed his gaze.

"It doesn't matter, I can always have them cleaned. Besides, if you stand up for much longer you're going to fall down."

He nodded his thanks and sank gratefully into the nearest chair.

"So what should I call you?" Yelana asked as she knelt by the fire.

The question knocked him off kilter. He had owned many names but none of them seemed to fit anymore. And his birth name, the one that should have stayed with him through everything, would mark him out as something terrible. *Traitor. Coward. Murderer.* Something these people would no longer be willing to help. He cleared his throat and gave her the most generic name he could think of.

"Jonah," he said. It was a name that belonged to no one. Something that marked him out as being nothing.

"Jonah …?" Her voice trailed off, her inflection turning

the name into a question, inviting further information from him.

"Just Jonah." His words sounded harsh to his own ears but if she noticed then she didn't seem offended.

"Well then, Jonah," she began again brightly. "How did you come to be outside on a night like this?"

He was saved from having to answer the question by Krenn's reappearance. Now that he could see him more clearly, the man estimated Krenn to be in his late twenties with a build that suggested he was used to hard work – likely in the fields, judging by the way he carried himself.

"The pantry isn't well stocked," Krenn said. "There were some herbs and I heated up some water to make tea. I hope that's alright?" He seemed to direct the question only to Yelana.

"Tea will be fine," she replied, smiling. "Krenn, this is Jonah," she continued, as smoothly as if she was introducing two acquaintances at a party.

Krenn nodded and handed Jonah a mug of tea. He didn't say anything but Jonah noticed the slight wrinkle of his nose as he leaned in.

"Jonah is going to be staying here tonight," Yelana said.

Jonah felt a jolt of surprise and he saw outright dismay on Krenn's face. He opened his mouth to protest but Yelana silenced him with one raised finger.

"I insist," she said in a tone of finality.

Jonah took a sip of his tea, not bothering to hide the grin that stretched across his face. *Little rich girl is used to getting what she wants, son. Better get used to it.*

"Right then," Krenn said. "I'll go and find somewhere for him to sleep."

Jonah took note of the barely concealed anger on Krenn's face as he left.

Yelana remained kneeling by the fire as Jonah cradled the hot mug of tea in his hands. She was angled slightly away from him and he found himself staring at the graceful arc of her neck, marvelling at anyone who would willingly turn their back on a stranger. He had a feeling though that she was not as unaware of his attention as she was pretending to be. There was a slight shakiness to her movements – as if she was forcing herself to move slowly to demonstrate her trust in him. Even from this angle he could see that her jaw was clenched tightly closed and he wondered whether she was afraid that her teeth would chatter. With Krenn out of the room she was all alone with him and Jonah allowed the fact of her closeness to intrude on his awareness.

Both Jonah and Yelana jumped slightly as Krenn re-entered the room. Yelana let out a small, nervous laugh and stood, brushing ash and dust from her skirt.

"There's a bed in the back room," Krenn said. "You might want to wash first," he added, disgust crossing his face again.

Jonah shifted uncomfortably and Yelana shot Krenn a reproachful look.

"It will help you get warm," he qualified, lamely.

Jonah nodded.

"Thank you," he said, stiffly.

"Down there to your right," Krenn said, pointing. "There's a bowl of water and some soap."

Jonah drained the last of his tea and stood slowly, testing his aching legs. He was about to leave the room when Yelana stopped him.

"You can leave your cloak here if you'd like. It'll dry faster by the fire."

She seemed to be staring at his chest and after a moment he realised why.

The dagger, he thought. The one he kept hidden in the lining of his cloak for emergencies. It was a nasty looking thing, covered in nicks and scratches. And probably even a little dried blood.

"No," he said quietly. "No thank you. I prefer to keep everything with me."

"Of course," she said lightly. But her eyes never moved from his chest.

Krenn gave him plenty of room as he passed.

Jonah rounded the corner and stood quietly, listening. He didn't have to wait long before they started talking about him.

"What are you doing?" Krenn demanded.

"I couldn't just let him leave."

Jonah could hear the reproach in Yelana's voice as she answered.

Jonah smiled and quietly left them to bicker.

Some time later, Jonah dropped what was left of the soap into the bowl of greyish water. He hadn't wanted to put his old clothes back on but no one had offered him anything else so he didn't really have a choice. For a moment he regretted not leaving his clothes to dry with Yelana – that way she would have had to offer him something else to wear. But that would have meant leaving his knives, along with the small pieces of broken glass, sharp bits of tin and trapping equipment along with them. Or worse, it would have meant emptying out his pockets in front of her. Krenn already considered him a threat and wanted him gone and even Yelana might have reconsidered letting him stay if she had seen what he was carrying around with him. So he unwillingly pulled his old clothes back on, trying not to wince as the stiffened fabric chafed against his newly scrubbed skin.

As he walked back into the main area of the cabin, Jonah could smell something cooking. His mouth began to water and he heard his stomach growl. He tried to remember how long it had been since he'd last eaten a hot meal.

Krenn was at the stove in the little kitchen area. Once again, Jonah wondered at his naivety in leaving his back turned to a stranger. Especially when they knew that he had a weapon on him. Jonah hadn't taken more than two steps before Krenn turned around, as if alerted to his presence. He saw the now familiar grimace pass across Krenn's face as he locked eyes with him. Krenn slowly dropped his gaze to take in Jonah's clothes. Without the stink of his own body odour to cover it up, Jonah could tell exactly how bad they smelt but he wasn't about to apologise to Krenn.

"I made soup," Krenn said, breaking the silence.

Jonah forced his face into what he hoped was an appropriate mask of gratitude.

"Thank you."

"The rain's stopped." Krenn's tone was deliberately neutral.

Jonah listened and realised that Krenn was right. The soft pattering against the roof had stopped.

"Yes," he agreed carefully.

"And it's getting late now," Krenn continued.

"Where's Yelana?" Jonah was surprised to find that he was suddenly uneasy without her presence. He scanned the kitchen and noticed that one of the knives was missing from the knife block. It was an effort to keep himself from touching his own knife, still tucked into the lining of his cloak.

Krenn shrugged.

Jonah spotted the knife, lying on the counter next to Krenn. He tried to move casually towards it but something in his movement must have given him away. Krenn took a single step to his left, effectively blocking his path.

"Where is she?" Jonah demanded.

Krenn met his gaze again and his eyes were cold.

"You should leave," he said quietly.

The sound of the cabin door slamming startled them both. A moment later, Yelana appeared.

"Oh good, the soup is ready. I'm starving." Her tone was bright. "Oh, I'm sorry, Jonah," she continued, contrition plain on her face. "I didn't mean literally 'starving' of course. That was very thoughtless of me. I can make you up a bag of food to take with you tomorrow. Unless you're planning on staying for more than one night?"

Behind him, Krenn made a strangled noise.

Jonah shook his head.

"No? Well then the least we can do is get some hot food into you tonight."

She sauntered over to the table and looked expectantly at Krenn.

It seemed obvious to Jonah that Yelana had money. It wasn't her easy offer to share her food or to let him stay at the cabin – in fact, if anything that marked her out as being different to the rest of her kind – it was in the way she spoke, her expectation that her every suggestion would be obeyed, her general sense of entitlement. Krenn on the other hand seemed a bit out of place. He was young and good-looking but it was obvious he didn't share Yelana's status. His clothes were well mended but not new, his hands were scrubbed but there was dirt under his fingernails. More importantly though, he was deferential to Yelana. However much he disagreed with her decisions tonight, he was never going to argue with her.

No, Jonah decided. *They're too mismatched to be a 'real' couple. Yelana is the daughter of somebody important – a noble perhaps? And Krenn is just the latest trinket to catch her eye.*

Idly, he wondered if anybody knew they were up here – and how much money Yelana's rich daddy would be willing to part with should she get herself into any trouble.

"Are you finished?" Yelana's question interrupted his train of thought.

He looked down at his empty bowl.

"There's some more in the pot. I'll get it for you." She held a hand out for his bowl.

"Don't you want any more?" he asked.

"No, I'm full and Krenn has hardly touched his anyway."

Jonah glanced at Krenn's bowl and realised Yelana was right.

Krenn gave a small sigh and began eating his soup, determinedly, one mouthful after another.

"There you go." Yelana placed the bowl back in front of Jonah and returned to her seat, watching him with bright eyes from behind her own empty bowl.

Only the rich can afford to go hungry.

Jonah finished his second bowl of soup and sat back, contented, in his chair. He could feel the warmth of the meal radiating out from his stomach and spreading through him. He felt pleasantly drowsy, as if he had drunk a glass of ale with his meal.

Across the table from him, Yelana yawned.

"Excuse me," she said, covering her mouth with her hand. "I seem to be tired all of a sudden."

"It's late," Krenn pointed out.

She yawned again.

"Yes. If you gentlemen would excuse me, I think I'm going to turn in for the night."

"We should probably all turn in," Krenn said, looking meaningfully at Jonah.

"Oh yes, Jonah, I'm sorry, did Krenn show you where your bed is?" Yelana asked.

"Down the hall to the right." The reluctance in Krenn's voice was plain.

Jonah stood up and stumbled slightly.

"Are you alright?" Yelana asked and he nodded.

"Just tired," he said.

Jonah took a tentative step forward, pleased that his legs held him and pointed his body towards the door.

"Goodnight then," he said awkwardly.

"Sleep well," Yelana replied.

Krenn said nothing.

Jonah found his room and pulled the door closed behind him, breathing a sigh of relief as he did so. He took his jacket off and dumped it beside the bed. His fingers fumbled clumsily with the laces on his boots and he frowned in frustration as he tried to make them work. After what seemed like an age but was probably only a few minutes, he managed to loosen his boots enough to pull them off. He didn't bother to remove the rest of his clothes before he lay down on the bed and fell asleep.

He woke with a bang several hours later. His head hurt and his mouth was dry. He still felt tired, as if his sleep hadn't refreshed him at all, despite the fact that he couldn't remember having woken in the night. Gradually he became aware of a strangeness in his own body, as if he was lying at an awkward angle. He tried to stretch and realised he couldn't move. Panic gripped him as he realised his wrists and ankles were bound. He pulled desperately at his binding and something hard and rough chafed against his skin.

"There's no point." Krenn's voice came out of the darkness, startling him.

"Krenn? What are you doing?"

Jonah heard the sound of a chair scraping slightly on the wooden floorboards and realised his captor was now standing. A moment later, Krenn's face loomed into view above him.

"You should have left when you had the chance." There was a note of something that almost sounded like regret in Krenn's voice.

Jonah latched onto it.

"I can leave now. Please – I'll go away and I'll never tell anyone about you."

Krenn laughed humourlessly. "Of course you won't. Who would you tell? Who would believe you?"

"Let me go, you sick bastard!" Jonah practically screamed.

"Krenn?" It was Yelana's voice, coming from the doorway. "What's happening in here?"

"Yelana!" Jonah cried. "Please, he's gone crazy."

"He's awake," Krenn said, his voice dull.

"I can hear that."

"Yelana?" Jonah turned it into a question this time.

"I'll be right with you, Jonah," she said. "Krenn, I think you should go."

"Go?" Krenn's voice was incredulous. "But…"

"Shh." She kissed him lightly on the cheek. "You trust me, don't you? You go. I'll take care of this whole mess and then join you later."

Jonah breathed a sigh of relief as he heard Krenn's footsteps retreating.

"Quick," he said urgently. "There's a knife in my cloak."

"This knife?" She held it up.

He blinked. "Yes. Use it to cut the rope and then we can both get out of here before he comes back."

She regarded the knife carefully, watching as the light from the rapidly rising sun glinted off the blade. A slow smile spread across her face.

"Why would I want to do that when I took so much trouble to get you here?"

"You? But Krenn…"

She laughed.

"Krenn has his uses, but he's never had an original idea in his life. He just does the heavy lifting so to speak."

Jonah's guts seemed to twist.

"Why?" he managed.

She laughed. "Why? Because I can. Because you're here, because no one will miss you. Because you were even good enough to bring your own knife. And there is one more reason." Slowly, she rolled her sleeve up and brought her wrist close to his face.

He squinted up at her in the half-light until his eyes adjusted enough for him to be able to see the outline of a mark on her wrist. He could easily have mistaken it for a birthmark – except that he had seen it before. The Tor'eath. The symbol of the death cult.

His heart sank and he felt a single tear run down his cheek.

"Oh cheer up. Didn't I give you a nice hot meal and a comfortable bed? Didn't I give you the best night you've had in ages? Honestly, some people are just so ungrateful." She grinned down at him and he wondered how he could possibly have missed the madness lurking behind those perfect blue eyes.

"Now, I'll do my best with this next part but you'll have to be patient with me. I've only done this a couple of times. I don't have a lot of practice yet."

"You don't have to do this. You could still let me go."

"Oh no, I can't do that. What are the chances that I came up here to this stranger's cabin to find you already here? It's serendipitous, you see. Like a gift from the gods." She leaned down and practically hissed at him; "And my gods will grant me such powers in return for your sacrifice." She laughed and her mask of sanity was instantly back in place. "This wasn't quite what Krenn had in mind for tonight but he knew the plans had changed as soon as he saw you. I'll find some other way to make it up to him." She flipped the knife in her hands once more and gave him a speculative look. "I don't suppose you'd like to tell me your name now?"

He shook his head and she shrugged.

"It doesn't really matter. You'll always be Jonah to me."

She raised the knife over her head.

He shut his eyes.

•

About Amy Wilson

Amy Wilson is a fantasy author based in the North East of England. She is currently working on her first full length novel whilst also training to climb Mount Kilimanjaro.

Find out more at www.6e.net/amywilson